A Midcoast Murder

A Midcoast Murder

By Stephen E. Stanley

Third Edition, 2011

Stonefield Publishing, 2009
stonefieldpublishing@gmail.com

Author's Note:

Anyone familiar with Bath, Maine will realize that I have taken great liberties with the geography and history of the town. There is no All Souls Church. I have used the historic Winter Street Church as the setting, though it is no longer an active place of worship.

This book is a work of fiction. All characters, names, institutions, and situations depicted in the book are the product of my imagination and not based on any persons living or dead. Anyone who thinks he or she is depicted in the book probably needs to get a life.

Special thanks to Cindy Stacy-Sevigny, who was my early reader and encouraged me through the early stages of the writing, and to Raymond Brooks for his support and patience.

Also by Stephen E. Stanley

MURDER IN THE CHOIR ROOM
A Jesse Ashworth Mystery

Chapter 1

"Life's a journey that is homeward bound..." –
Herman Melville

The tide was full and the waves were washing up on the white sands of the beach. As I looked back I could see the waves washing away the footprints I had left in the sand. It was the perfect metaphor. Having taught literature for over thirty years, symbolism had been my life. The tides of time washing away my imprints seemed to say it all. Change was coming; I could feel it in the air. I don't know how I knew it at the time, but I needed to move on in my life.

It seemed like only yesterday that I was looking forward to the possibilities of all that life offered. I could be anything I wanted, or so I thought. When I was a kid growing up in Maine I wanted to be a forest ranger. I thought I'd look great in a really cool forest ranger uniform. I planned to live in a log cabin in the wilds of Maine's outback, spend winters in front of a roaring fire whenever I wasn't out doing whatever it is that forest rangers do.

Later I discovered that I'm not really all that fond of being out in the hot sun all summer or the winter cold. I still love the outdoors, but I prefer seeing it from a lounge chair at a five-star resort with pool boys bringing me umbrella drinks.

1

There were no pool boys in sight, and I thought the chances of having an umbrella drink on this deserted Maine beach were very remote. A cold wind came up and it was time to head back home and get ready for work tomorrow.

. . . .

It was eight o'clock the next morning, and I was standing in the middle of a room holding a human skull while everyone had horrified looks on their faces. Who says dreams don't come true?

I had everyone's full attention now as I slowly rotated the skull in my hands and closely examined the skull. I could tell that there was tension in the room.

"As Hamlet holds the skull of Yorick, act five takes on a tragic tone." I took a deep breath, looked around the classroom and continued. "As you will see when you finish reading act five of *Hamlet* for homework."

There were groans at the word homework, but I figured they would get over it. The bell rang and my students filed out the door.

"Nice skull, Mr. Ashworth," said one of my twelfth-graders as he passed by my desk. I watched the students disappear down the hallway.

It was my free period, so I had no students in my room for the next fifty minutes or so. Rhonda Shepard waltzed into my classroom, coffee cup in hand and took a seat.

"I just dropped off my intent to retire letter to the Amazing Asshole," she announced. "I wanted you to hear it first. Of course I told the Amazing Asshole that I didn't want anybody to know, which

Stephen E. Stanley

means I've got less than thirty minutes before he blabs it all over the school."

The Amazing Asshole was our nickname for Dick Bentley, our principal. As you can imagine, a name like Dick Bentley gave us a lot to work with, and as for the nickname, use your imagination.

"Who's your friend?" asked Rhonda, indicating the skull on the desk.

"It's a sandstone cast I borrowed from the biology department."

"Hamlet?"

"What else?"

Rhonda nodded.

"This is the first I've heard of retirement. When did this come about?" I asked. I had been teaching English literature across the hall from Rhonda for over thirty years. We had become friends and seen each other through divorces (hers), breakups (mine), failed diets (both of us) and quite a few laughs, mostly at the expense of others!

"I turned sixty yesterday, and I want to do something else before I die. I don't want to end up like Russ Davis." Russ Davis, a 52-year-old math teacher, dropped dead in the middle of cafeteria duty last year. I thought it could be much worse, at least he wasn't on bathroom duty, or even worse, sitting on the crapper in the men's room. I think dying on lunch duty trumps dying on a toilet any day; at least your pants aren't around your ankles.

"Good point," I agreed. "I tried to call you this weekend to wish you a happy birthday, but I got no answer."

"I was away for the weekend, and you'll never guess where!"

3

"With a man?" I asked.

"I wish!" said Rhonda as she took a sip of coffee. She can get more mileage from a cup of coffee than anyone I know.

"Okay where?"

"The Maine coast," she answered. "Bath, actually"

"Get out of here!"

"I knew you grew up there, so I was curious to see the place you talk about now and then. It's really much lovelier than you make it out to be."

"So did you like it?" I asked.

"I not only liked it, I put a deposit on a condo."

I was speechless for a moment or two. "Okay then, I need some coffee before I can deal with this." I walked to the teachers' room, poured some coffee, checked my mailbox and headed back to my room. I took a gulp of coffee.

"Let me get this straight," I said as I sat down and took another gulp of coffee. "You turned sixty, drove up the coast to Bath, Maine, where you know not a soul, bought a condo, came back to New Hampshire, walked into the Amazing Asshole's office and told him you are retiring at the end of June. Is that pretty much it?"

"Pretty much," she answered.

"And you don't think this behavior is a little out of character for you?" I asked. Rhonda had worked at the same job and lived in the same house for as long as I can remember. She was what I always called "settled" into life.

"There's more," she added after a few seconds of silence.

"Oh, boy!"

"I signed a lease with an option to buy a shop in the downtown section of town."

"What?" I was too stunned to speak.

"I've always wanted to be my own boss," she said rather lamely.

The bell rang for the next class period and we both got up.

"See you at lunch!" said Rhonda as she headed into her classroom.

I didn't know it then, but Rhonda's decisions would also alter my life in unimaginable ways.

. . . .

When I was a kid, the five and dime store sat on the corner of Front and Center Street. Diagonally across from it was Hallet's Drug Store. Various family businesses filled the surrounding stores. Now the streets are lined with antique shops and boutiques, with a few restaurants snuggled in between them. Yet, on the whole, things look very much the same as when I was in school. Much of the hardscrabble edge has worn off and been replaced by a more genteel patina, due in part to the influx of yuppies and the exodus of the working class. But mostly anyone who grew up here would recognize the town.

Like most local boys growing up here I had the choice of sticking around and ending up working for the Bath Iron Works, or move away, go to college, and work somewhere else. I chose to leave right after high school, attend college, and teach high school English in New Hampshire.

I hadn't planned to retire early, and I certainly had no plans to move back here. In fact, if it hadn't been for Rhonda Shepard, I most certainly wouldn't have given it a thought. I was just barely eligible for early retirement myself, so I began to think about it.

I spent several weeks in July helping her move in, set up her shop, and rediscovered the town and a few old friends from high school. Much had changed and much had stayed the same. For whatever reason, I began to make connections in the place where I grew up.

Labor Day came and I went back to school in New Hampshire. Rhonda wasn't the only teacher to have retired from the English department and as a result some energetic new teachers, most of whom were born several years after I started teaching, surrounded me. They were all nice enough, but I missed my old friends.

This was the last year of our union contract and the school board was making it clear that teachers cost the city too much and that retirement benefits needed to be trimmed. Did I want to take a chance on sticking around another year or two with the possibility of a reduced retirement package or take early retirement? I wasn't sure and so I avoided thinking about it as much as possible.

Finally the breaking point came in December at a faculty meeting where it was announced that the school board had decided that every teacher in the district would be teaching only what was on the curriculum, and all teachers who were teaching the same subject would we covering the same materials on the same day. This, they reasoned, was the best way to improve student scores on standardized tests.

I had always taken pride in the fact that I was able to modify my lessons to the needs of my students. Now I would have to teach material to the students whether they were ready or not. The next day I dropped off my intent to retire to the Amazing Asshole.

And so here I am on Memorial Day weekend with most of my worldly goods packed into the one-car detached garage on Sagamore Street while workman renovate the 1925 bungalow I bought one weekend last month after a minor bout of insanity. On Monday night I will have to go back to finish the last three weeks of school, close on the New Hampshire house, and start a new life.

We were in the front yard and Argus was pulling me along on his leash when Rhonda's car pulled up and she yelled "Coffee!" as she stepped out of her Honda Civic. Argus made a beeline to Rhonda with his pug dog tail wagging furiously.

"How did you get them to work on a holiday weekend?" she asked as she looked at the workmen on the roof. I noticed she also brought along a bag of pastries. Good girl!

"Nothing I did. They must have a lot of jobs lined up for the rest of the summer because here they are!" I replied. We headed for the picnic table under the tree in the back yard.

More workmen arrived and headed into the house with some serious looking tools. "So what are you going to do today?" she asked. "It looks like there won't be much room in there for you with all the work being done."

I looked around at the overgrown and neglected yard. "I thought I'd work on the yard, dig up some turf and get a start on the vegetable garden, and after that I'll begin planting some perennials out in the front yard." I took a very yummy-looking Danish pastry out of the bag and began eating it.

Rhonda held up three fingers. "Three more weeks!" she said between bites of a cinnamon roll "Are you ready?"

"I guess," I replied. "How did you feel about retirement?"

"It was like the end of any school year. I was really tired and just looked forward to summer. Then I came here, got a new life, and ever since I've been too busy having fun to give it much thought."

I watched some workmen haul out some ugly pink tile from one of the bathrooms and throw it into a dumpster. "Well, I hope this new-life-thing works out okay. I'm not sure yet." Just then two more workmen came out with an old three burner electric range and threw in a big dumpster.

"Jesse," she looked straight at me, "it's going to be just fine. All of it. The house, retirement and moving back here, after all this is your hometown. Anyone who can stare down a class of twelfth graders can handle anything." Rhonda looked at her watch. "I've got to go open the shop. Another day and another dollar and I mean that literally!" Actually Rhonda's gift shop was doing very well since she had expanded to include an Internet catalog. "Come on down for lunch."

"Okay, I'll be down around noon."

As it turned out I never made it for lunch.

Chapter 2

Ever have that feeling that you are being watched? I had it as I began digging out the garden. My grandmother was a Spiritualist and so I had grown up around people who regularly talked to the dead. Feelings that you were being watched were fairly normal. Growing up I realized that I had inherited my grandmother's highly developed intuition. As an adult I tried to tell myself that intuition was nothing but imagination, but sometimes the old family gift kicked in when I least expected it. Like now!

Of course stupid, I thought to myself, you are being watched. There are probably ten workers at the house who think you are a complete idiot for fixing this place up. But when I looked around none of them were visible and the feeling of being watched seemed to be coming from another direction.

Argus was napping under a tree on the blanket I put out for him, and he was snoring away unconcerned. I continued to dig.

About half an hour later I had a fairly good-sized garden patch dug up, plus two old beer bottles, three large rocks, a rusted peace medallion from the 1960's, three bottle caps, and a few plastic beads. I stuck the peace medallion in my pocket to polish up later. I still had the eerie feeling of being watched as I continued to dig. Argus was awake now and watching me with one eye. My shovel hit another rock just as Argus starting barking. I moved the shovel around the rock to get better leverage, but as I looked closer I saw it wasn't a rock at all. I jumped back, fumbled for my cell phone and dialed 911.

"Um, hi, I'm Jesse Ashworth at 37 Sagamore Street, and I think I just found a body in my back yard!"

. . . .

My backyard was cordoned off with yellow crime tape and a small crowd had gathered. The workmen had given up any pretense to working and the New England Cable News had just finished taping. Great! My students would see this back in Manchester, and I could pretty much toss out my lesson plan for Tuesday. I couldn't wait for their questions, "So did you kill him, Mr. Ashworth?"

The first policeman to arrive told me I probably had dug up an old Indian grave. I had to point out that Native Americans most likely didn't wear polka dot polyester. As I was waiting earlier for someone to show up I moved some dirt around and saw a pink and yellow piece of cloth. I must have been in shock because my first thought was polyester isn't biodegradable. My second thought was who would wear something that ugly? My third thought was even more humiliating; something along the line of "I wouldn't be caught dead in a fabric like that!" Fortunately before I could think of any more profound observations the police showed up.

Don't ask me how Rhonda found out, but she showed up with a bag of burgers and fries, her solution for trauma. She and I were at the picnic table with Argus, and the guys from the state crime lab were sifting through my backyard, and more people arrived to see the commotion.

"Man in uniform," Rhonda whispered as a tall, good-looking policeman approached. I noticed that he had more stripes and braid than most officers. There was something vaguely familiar about him.

"Ashes, can't you come to town just once without causing trouble?" Ashes was my high school nickname. Nobody had called me that in thirty-five years.

"Tim, is that really you?" Tim Mallory had been one of my high school friends. I did a quick visual inventory: my age, full head of hair, no wedding ring, big shoulders, and no beer gut. Tim had always wanted to be a cop. I guess he got his wish.

"I'm the police chief here," he replied. "And what the hell is this all about?"

I explained about buying the house and digging the garden and finding the skull.

"Christ, it could only happen to you. Do you remember the Halloween séance you hosted back when we were seniors? It really freaked me out."

A group of us gathered on Halloween for a séance. Just as I called on the spirits, all the lights on the street went out and the single candle in the middle of the table flared up.

"I'm sure it all was a coincidence. After all the power was always going out," I said.

"It really freaked us out, if you remember."

"How long before all this," I swept my hand at the investigation team, "goes away?

"I'm not sure. I'll go ask," Tim said.

Rhonda had been silent throughout the conversation. As Tim strode away she whispered "Hot!" Then she looked at me and said, "I'll want

11

the details of the Halloween story, and," she added, "you never told me about him."

. . . .

By the end of Saturday I was exhausted. The remodeling and repairs on the house were bad enough, but the added events were too much. That evening in Rhonda's guest room I got undressed without putting my clothes away, crawled into bed and slept. It wasn't until Sunday morning that I began to pick up my clothes and put them away. As I was going through my jeans pocket I found the peace medallion I had uncovered in the garden the day before. I had forgotten about it in all the chaos of the day.

I went into Rhonda's kitchen and put on the coffee, fed Argus and took him outside. When Rhonda came down I handed her the medallion. "I dug this up a yesterday. Do you think it might be connected to the body?"

"And good morning to you, too!" She looked at the medallion. "It needs to be cleaned up. I've got some jewelry cleaner upstairs. Let me go try it."

I made breakfast while Rhonda cleaned the medallion. Since I was staying with Rhonda until my bungalow was livable, I was paying her back by doing the cooking. Rhonda claims she doesn't cook. I, on the other hand, enjoy doing it. Argus was under my feet as I cooked, hoping some morsel would magically fall to the floor. I know Rhonda loves Argus, but I noticed that she always covers up the chairs and sofa when I come for the weekend. I couldn't blame her. Only uranium has a longer half-life than pug hair.

"I cleaned it up as best as I could, but there is still some rust and corrosion on it." Rhonda passed me the medallion as I handed her a plate of eggs, bacon and blueberry pancakes. "Oh my God this looks good," she said.

"There something inscribed on the back," I said as I tried to read it. "Do you have a magnifying glass?"

"It's in the third drawer over there."

I found the magnifying glass and sat down with my breakfast. I looked at the back of the medallion and could just make out the date "1969."

"Do you think I should tell someone?" I asked Rhonda. "It was some distance from where I found the skull."

Rhonda looked at me carefully and replied, "You never know. It might be a good idea to call the police. Or even better, you can call the police chief. And by the way, you were going to tell me about him."

"There's not much to tell." I said as I devoured my pancakes. I was very hungry this morning. "We went to high school together. I lived in the north end, and he lived in the south end. He was a football player and I was in the band. Back then they always placed us in alphabetical order. I was an A and he was an M. So out paths didn't cross often. We hung out some in the summer, but then we were a small class compared to Manchester's Amoskeag High School."

"What type of girls did he date?" Rhonda was always looking at the romantic side of life, hence her three marriages and numerous relationships.

"Well," I had to think. It had been a long time. "Mostly he went out with Judy Blair. She was one of those hair-sprayed cheerleaders who though she was beautiful and smart, but in reality she was neither. In fact we had elected her class bitch, which the yearbook refused to print.

"Then after graduation I didn't see him again until our fifth-year reunion. He brought his new wife with him. She hated us and barely spoke at all. They left early that night."

"That's it?" she said. "I thought you had a good story from the way you two greeted each other."

"Nope, that's just the Maine way. Friends for life. Even if fifty years passes we treat each other as if we saw them just yesterday," I replied.

"Do you think he likes older women?" she asked.

"I think after dealing with the women in his life, he probably doesn't like women at all." I said. "His mother was a real harridan, too."

She sighed, "All the good ones are either married, priests or...."

"I know." I interrupted. "So what are you doing today?" I tried to change the subject as I took the dirty dishes and put them in the dishwasher.

"Not so fast. I want to know about the Halloween séance."

"Not much of a story. It was back in my high school and some of the kids were into tarot cards and Ouija boards. I'd watched my grandmother have séances as a kid, so I decided to have one for kicks. We sat around with our hands on the table. I played the medium and just as I called upon the spirits the lights went out. One girl screamed because she thought a cold hand had brushed her face. It was nothing but a power failure and teenage imagination. We had a lot of power outages at school, and the kids were watching *Dark Shadows* on TV and getting some really weird ideas.

She laughed," Well, that must explain some of the blackouts we've been in. By the way, I'm going to church this morning. Do you want to come?"

"You're kidding right?" After several attempts to be a churchgoer, I now regarded organized religion on the same level as small pox.

"Not that church!" she emphasized. We had both belonged to the same denomination and had sworn off priests, bishops, and other superfluous flotsam. We now called ourselves recovering Episcopalians. "I'm going to All Souls Church. You know, the one that looks like a picture post card? I've been going for a while and I like it"

"You have?" This was the first I had heard about any church.

"Yes, ever since I moved here. I went at first because I thought it would be a way to meet people in the community, but then I started to really like it."

"What the hell. Let me leave a message for Tim about the medallion and I'll go." I had always been curious to see the inside of the building. After all I had just found a body in my back yard, so maybe I could use a little church. Still it was a toss-up as to which I prefer to do: have a root canal with no Novocain, or listen to a bunch of other peoples' holy opinions.

"I'll drive," was all I said.

Church wasn't all that bad despite my misgivings. The sanctuary was lofty and light-filled. There was the lighting of the candles, some readings, hymns and a sermon. We ended with a thoughtful meditation. The theme of the service was personal redemption. No one tried to save me or threaten me with hell fire, so I didn't suffer the claustrophobia I usually get in church services. We stayed for coffee and I met some of the people. They all seemed to know Rhonda, so I guessed she had been a regular for a while. Who knew?

On our way back to the condo we stopped by my house. The workers were there even though it was Sunday. The roof was being replaced and the painters had begun to paint the house yellow. Rhonda had once pointed out to me that every house I liked was yellow, so I decided to have this one be my yellow house. I had hacked down some brush from the front yard and hauled away tons for junk and the curb appeal of the house was beginning to show. The yellow crime tape was still up in the backyard. I truly hoped that when the insulation guys came to insulate the walls, that they wouldn't find anybody buried in the studs.

"I think this is going to be great when it's fixed up," said Rhonda. She always tries to make me see the bright side.

"What was I thinking? I had a perfectly fine house back in Manchester."

'Yes," said Rhonda, "and it's time to move on. Look how much money you got from the sale and look at the great price you got for this place. Even with the renovations you'll have money left over and a much nicer house."

"Okay, let's get out of here. I'll make us some lunch and take Argus for a walk."

Rhonda decided to walk the dog with me. Just as we got to the end of the street a police car pulled up and Tim stepped out.

"Hey Ashes, I got your message." Tim bent down to play with Argus. Argus was beside himself with excitement, tail wagging and he was barking up a storm.

"Hi Tim," Funny, but I couldn't think of much to say as I looked at him. My mind went blank.

"You look well, Jesse."

"You too, Tim." He really didn't look his age. Good genes.

"Are you going to the alumni dinner?" Every year the Morse High School Alumni Association puts on a dinner for the graduating class. It also provided for the reunions of all the classes at five-year intervals. This was our thirty-fifth reunion year.

"I sent in my money, but I'm not sure if I want to go or not," I said.

"I have to go. My daughter is graduating this year. And," he reminded me, "It's our thirty-fifth reunion."

"Didn't I meet your wife at our fifth-year reunion?" I didn't elaborate about what I really remembered about her. "She was a nurse if I remember correctly. Is she still nursing?"

"Nursing a big time grudge, I'm sure." Tim answered. "She's living in Florida with her new husband. If she's doing anything it's casting spells and cavorting with the devil."

"Double, double toil and trouble," I quoted from *Macbeth*.

"Fire burn and cauldron bubble," echoed Tim.

"Open locks…" I started

"…Whoever knocks!" finished Tim.

"By the pricking of my thumb…"

"…Something wicked this way comes." We both started laughing.

"I still remember those lines from old lady LaFond's English class," I said.

Rhonda cleared her throat. I had forgotten she was there.

"Tim, this is…" and suddenly my mind went blank again and I couldn't for the life of me come up with her name. I guess the thirty-five year leap in memory was too much for my brain. I looked at Tim and we both started to laugh again.

"Rhonda Shepard. And this asshole who's having a memory lapse used to be my best friend." She put out her hand for Tim. "I was with Jesse yesterday when you came by."

"Really?" said Tim. "I don't remember seeing you." Rhonda rolled her eyes at me.

"Oh," I suddenly remembered why he was here. I took the medallion out of my pocket. "I found this when I was digging yesterday and forgot about it in the excitement." I handed over to Tim. "It looks like someone engraved 1969 on the back of it."

"I'll give it to the crime boys in Augusta and see if they can make a connection." Tim took the medallion. "It's nice to meet you." He said to Rhonda as he flashed a smile. "Keep in touch Ashes," he said to me and then strode off to his car.

"Hot!" said Rhonda as she watched Tim get into the car.

"You said that before," I reminded her.

"No one past fifty should be that good looking," she said.

"Age is just a number." I had started to use that cliché a lot since my last birthday.

"Well," said Rhonda. "I felt completely invisible. And you" she continued, "couldn't even remember my name! I swear you two turned into teenage boys before my very eyes."

"Sorry, for a minute it felt like I was back in high school. I think the trip down memory road is going to be a long journey," I was joking. I had no idea then just how long a trip it would be.

Chapter 3

Memorial Day turned out to be a washout. It started to rain late Sunday night and continued into Monday. I drove back to New Hampshire on Monday with Argus curled up in the seat beside me. I can never figure out why he gets so excited about going for a ride when, as soon as we get underway, he circles in the seat three times, lies down, and snores until we get home.

Home! I had no home! Right now I was living in a house that someone else had bought. All my things were in a garage in Maine, next to a house that was undergoing so many repairs that I couldn't even sleep there. And now I had to finish out the school year in a house that only had a mattress on the floor, a folding chair to sit on, and a crate for Argus.

Being questioned about finding a skeleton in my backyard by the authorities was nothing like the grilling I got on Tuesday by my students. As I described in detail what I found, I added a few gory details of my own invention. They hung onto my every word. If only they listened to my lectures on *Hamlet* with such rapt attention!

"So did you kill him Mr. Ashworth?" laughed Bert Conner from his seat in the front of the room. I put down my book, walked slowly over to him and put my hands on either side of his desk, looked him in the eyes and said, "You see Bert, he didn't do his homework. These things happen. Did you do your homework Bert?"

"Yes sir," he replied. Silently he pushed his homework forward.

The bell rang and the students ran out into the hall. The school day was over and I sat at my desk to process the events of the last few days. Things had finally settled down as the state crime lab people left late in the day on Saturday. The media reported that a new homeowner who had been digging in his backyard found a skeleton. Authorities believed that it was most likely the remains of a woman, cause of death unknown, and that the remains had been buried for several decades.

Several days later it began to dawn on me that I was teaching twentieth century poets for the last time. I was sad and feeling some sense of loss, but also I had the increasing feelings of freedom. I was, after all, retiring early, some fifteen years before the typical retirement age. Okay, so maybe it's only ten years, but still I was feeling the winds of change in my face and it felt great.

It was a short week because of the Monday holiday and, as usual for high school, we had end of the year assemblies for the students and the school days went by quickly. The students talked about the body in my backyard for a full two days and then, as usually happen with teenagers, something more exciting came along to grab their attention.

On Thursday night my cell phone rang. It was Tim. "Hi Ashes, I just called to give you an update. The crime boys were able to salvage some clothing from the scene and they think the medallion might be related. The year seems to have been engraved with some type of hand tool because it looks like a homemade job. They are checking the dental records right now to see if there is a match up with any missing person reports, some going years back. They think it's foul play for sure."

"Well," I replied, "I'm sure she didn't commit suicide and then bury herself."

"It could have been an accident and then someone tried to cover it up. You never know." Then he continued, "Are you going Saturday to the dinner? I have to go and I'd like to have somebody there I know."

"Come on, you must know everyone in town," I said, but I was glad he wanted me there.

"Knowing and liking are two very different things, okay?"

"In that case count me in. I have to go check on the house repairs this weekend so I'll be there anyway."

"Great! See you there. Six o'clock." And then he hung up. What was all that about, I wondered?

The worse thing about house remodeling is that usually you have to live there while it's being done. I was lucky this time; most of the work was done during the week while I was away. Here it was June and finally the house was almost finished. I had a new roof, new windows, insulation, and fresh paint inside and outside, and new plumbing and electrical. Everything was move-in ready except for the kitchen. It was the kitchen that was almost the deal breaker for this house.

I had no intention of moving, at first. But I had such a good time visiting with Rhonda during the summer that I actually wondered what it would be like to live where I grew up. One of Rhonda's condo neighbors, Robin Jeffers, was a real estate agent and offered to take us around and show us a few listings "just for fun."

None of the houses we saw were remarkable until we came to the house on Sagamore Street. I thought I knew Bath very well, but I had never been on this street before. It was a short dead-end street off another short street. The lot was large, just the right amount of sun and shade. The house sat up on a hill with a great view in all directions. It was a 1925 one-story bungalow, and very much in the Maine fashion, it was plain on the outside and finely detailed on the inside. It had a wide front porch and a screen porch on the back. There was a fenced in yard for Argus and plenty of room for flowers and even a small vegetable garden. It even had a small tool shed. What man doesn't like a tool shed?

From the porch I could see all the way to the river. Over the door was a weathered sign that read "Eagle's Nest." It was the fashion in Maine during the 1920's and '30's to give names to houses. The sign looked old enough to be original to the house.

The front door opened into the living room. It had a high ceiling, large windows and a fireplace. There was a hardwood floor and crown molding. It needed some paint, but it was easy to see the fine detail and craftsmanship. A large archway led into a small alcove, just right for a little office or TV room. It had great period lighting fixtures and a window seat. I was already calculating an offering price, but then we stepped into the kitchen,

"What the hell is this?" I asked. It was a big room but mostly empty. There was an electric stove from the 1950's with only three burners. It looked like it hadn't been cleaned since Kennedy was shot.

There was a copper tone refrigerator and a metal sink cabinet that had been painted pink and nothing else in the room! No cupboards, no cabinets, nothing! What made it even worse was the wallpaper. It was decorated, if you can call it that, with red and green teapots. What the hell was up with that?

"It is a little basic," said Robin, "but a single guy like you probably doesn't cook much." I let the sexist remark go, but mentally deducted ten thousand dollars from my offer just for the annoyance.

"Well as a matter of fact, not only do I cook, but I've been to culinary school in Paris and on occasion I've worked as a chef." It was mostly true. I did go to culinary school, even though it was only for a six-week term. Chef might be a stretch too, but I had been a cook on a sailing yacht during a few summer vacations.

"Then this is a great opportunity to have the kitchen built to your standards." She had me on that one.

The two bedrooms were both good sized and had closets and good ventilation. The master bedroom had a private bath, but the guest bathroom had a tub, with no shower, so that would have to be fixed also.

I wrote a figure on a piece of paper and handed it to her. "This is what I'm prepared to pay. The house is in terrible shape and will have to be repaired from top to bottom. In fact this can only be described as a tear-down! It's a take it or leave it deal. Don't annoy me with a counter offer because this is my one and only offer for this dump." I was some tough guy! Actually the figure was so low I thought I'd never hear from her again.

"Okay Jesse, I'll have to get back to you."

"The only word I want to hear from you is yes or no." I said and then stomped out of the house.

Later that day my cell phone rang. "Jesse, the place is yours!" said the voice. What had I done?

. . . .

There is no place more beautiful than coastal Maine in June. Everything is in bloom; the air is fresh from the sea, and the light is fantastic. Artists have always been drawn to coastal Maine by the rich colors of nature and the light than illuminates the rugged landscape. On this June morning I was slowly moving boxes from the garage and unpacking them in the house. All the windows were open because the house still smelled of paint and polish. The work was slow because I kept taking breaks on the screen porch. Argus was following me around and wouldn't let me out of his sight. Dogs don't like their routines upset, and they certainly don't like packing and unpacking.

Argus heard footsteps on the porch before I did and ran to the door just as the doorbell rang. Funny but it occurred to me that I had never heard the doorbell, in fact I don't think I had even noticed if there was a doorbell or not. Through the screen door I saw this quite elderly couple standing there.

"Good morning," I said rather cautiously. I hoped they weren't carrying religious literature.

"Good morning. We're the Lowells and we live next door. I'm John and this is Dorothy."

25

"Hi, I'm Jesse Ashworth. Do come in." Dorothy handed me a plate of cookies that were obviously freshly baked. "Would you like some coffee?" I asked. "The coffee pot is about the only thing in my kitchen right now." Fortunately the living room furniture had arrived from the store several days earlier. I indicated that they should make themselves comfortable and moved some boxes from the sofa to the floor. I went into the kitchen to brew a fresh pot of coffee. There seemed to be something familiar about them, but I couldn't quite figure out why.

I returned with three coffee mugs having found them in a box marked 'kitchen misc.'

"We're thrilled that someone bought the house and fixed it up," said John. "It's always been an eyesore. As long as we've lived here it's just been renters, usually only for a few months and then it stands vacant for months and then someone else moves in."

"This is very nice and cozy," Dorothy remarked as she looked around.

"Are you from away?" John asked as he looked at me curiously. There are two types of people in Maine. You are either born here or you are from "away" which is anywhere in the world except Maine.

"No, I was born on the coast and grew up here. I graduated from Morse High. I spent a few years away as a teacher, but I came back here to retire. Well, actually I won't retire until school is finished next week." In Maine thirty years qualifies as a few years.

Dorothy took up the conversation. "I'm a retired teacher, too. What school did you go to?" Since there was only one high school and one middle school I knew she had to be asking about elementary schools, as there were a number of them.

"Huse School," I answered. What was with all the questions I wondered, and then it hit me.

"Mrs. Lowell? You were my third grade teacher!" By a quick reckoning in my head I figured she must be about two hundred years old. She seemed very old to me when I was in third grade, but she probably was no more than thirty, if that. I guess my math was off by about a hundred and thirty years.

We had a pleasant chat. I filled them in on my life since high school. I gave them a tour of the house, such as it was and then they excused themselves.

I worked the rest of the morning setting out perennials in the garden and then, because it was getting close to lunch time, I went to Amato's sandwich shop and picked up two Italian sandwiches to take to Rhonda's shop. Maine Italian sandwiches are unique. Other places claim to sell Italian subs, but they are nothing like these. Some small grocery stores in Portland owned by Italian immigrants began making sandwiches for the shipyard workers in World War I. The simple ingredients include a soft roll, ham, salami, cheese, tomato, onion, green pepper, black olives, freshly ground pepper, and olive oil. Anyone who makes it with a hard roll, or God forbid, lettuce has, in my opinion, created culinary blasphemy.

I pulled into a parking space on Front Street and went into Rhonda's shop. She had named the store Erebus, which was a name from Greek mythology. She sold unusual gift items and had recently added some New Age products; it was these things that really helped her business take off.

"Food!" she cried as I put the sandwiches on the counter. "What was your week like?"

"Busy." I gave her the rundown on the last week of classes and how I was ready for next week's final exams and the ending of the school year. I told her about all the work that was done on the house while I was in New Hampshire, and about my neighbor being my third grade teacher. "That's about it." I concluded.

"Oh," I added. "I'm going to my thirty-fifth high school reunion tonight."

"Baby!" she teased. "I was already teaching high school back then. And it wasn't my first year either. I thought you weren't going to go to your reunion"

"Well, Tim Mallory called this week and asked me if I was going. I guess he wanted a friendly face there."

"What's with that?" asked Rhonda as she gave me her usual eye roll.

"I'm not really sure. I expect it's going to be mind numbingly boring."

If I was expecting to be bored that night I was in for a very big surprise.

Chapter 4

Argus woke me up from my afternoon nap, so I got up, fed him and then took him for a walk in the neighborhood. John Lowell was out weeding his lawn and waved as we went by. I had about an hour to shower and get ready to go out to the alumni dinner. I wasn't sure what to wear because it was close to ninety degrees out and a tie and jacket wouldn't do in this weather. I figured dressy casual would be fine.

At six o'clock I rolled into the middle school parking lot. The middle school had a larger gym than the high school for the gathering. We were to have a class meeting in room 511 before we marched into the gym by class. The oldest class was first and the graduating class last. The school didn't look like it had changed much since the time when I went to school, back when it was known as the junior high.

I had no trouble finding room 511, but as I stepped into the room, I thought I had made a mistake; it was filled with old people! I looked at the hand-drawn sign on the door. Sure enough it was my class. I spotted Tim Mallory sitting over in the corner and waving to me. He didn't look old and neither did the group of people he was sitting with. I guess not everyone ages at the same rate, or if they do some of these people had badly abused themselves.

"Hi Jesse," said the blonde sitting by Tim. It was Sue Abbot. She and I sat near each other in most classes.

"Hi Sue," I responded. Sue was always friendly and honest. In fact she was chosen as most likable in our class.

"Hey, Jesse Ashworth., do you still talk to the dead?" It took me a moment to place the little round woman who had spoken, but the bitchy look I got from her told me it could only be Judy Blair.

"Sure Judy, I'll talk to you!" I responded. Everyone in the group laughed. Judy laughed too, but if looks could kill...

Just then the class president called the meeting to order. At roll call we each gave our name and how far we had to travel to this event. We had a good turnout of over seventy out of the original one hundred and ten. Some lived too far away to come, some didn't care to come, and I suspected some couldn't come because they had taken the final dirt bath!

The intercom crackled and we were called to the gym to get ready to march in. As we lined up single file, I swear Tim pushed me in front of him so that I would be between him and Judy. I gave Tim a look and he leaned into me and whispered, "Make her go away!" Okay, so the evening was going to have some entertainment value after all. We chatted up and down the line until we got to the lobby to wait our turn.

The class of 1955 had the largest turnout. They must have been a big class at the height of the baby boomer period. They were all fit and trim and looked healthy. The class of 1940 was the oldest class to have a whole table for themselves. All the survivors of the classes before 1940 were gathered at one long table in front of the stage. They ranged from the class of 1928 to 1939. When you manage to outlive most of your class, then you get invited every year, not just every five years. Lucky them!

When we graduated back in the day, we were given a paper plate with cold cuts and potato salad. Dinner had been kicked up a notch now; we had broiled chicken and rice with vegetables. I sat between Tim and Judy and across from Sue Abbot and high school sweethearts Bill and Becky Simpson.

Every time a class was introduced we were obliged to clap, which was great, otherwise we would have had to listen to Bill and Becky talk about their kids and their new granddaughter. When the graduating class was introduced we all stood and clapped. Tim pointed out his daughter Jessica in a red dress as she turned and waved to him.

"How come she's living with you and not her mother?" I asked. There is nothing like getting to the point with a personal question.

"She thinks her mother is a bitch," he answered. Score one for the daughter!

The dinner continued and each class was introduced and a spokesperson got up to speak. The only excitement came when they made the introductions at the survivor's table. The class of 1928's sole remaining member was Beatrice LaFond.

"Isn't that old lady LaFond, our English teacher?" I asked the table.

"Oh, my God!" exclaimed Becky Simpson. "I thought she was dead!"

"Hard to tell from here," I remarked.

"Maybe you could talk to her, Jesse, if she is dead." snarled Judy. We hadn't nicknamed her Bitch Blair for nothing!

"She must be in her late nineties," I said, ignoring Judy's comment.

"Or older," Tim added. "I thought she was very old when we had her."

"She was a terror," Sue said.

"I hated her, stupid woman!" said Becky with a vehemence that I had never seen. Her husband Bill looked shocked.

"Where's your husband Judy? asked Bill, just to change the subject. We had heard that she married a guy with money.

"Dead!" she replied.

"Oh, I'm sorry," said Sue.

"Don't be. He was an asshole!" Judy almost spit as she said it. There wasn't a lot to say after that. Death can be a real conversation stopper.

Dessert was served and the president of the graduating class got up to speak. The dinner was over. People got up to talk to people they knew from other classes. Jessica Mallory made her way to her father and Tim introduced me as his old high school friend.

"You don't look old enough to be in this class," she said to me. Score two for the kid.

"Some of us stay in shape," said Tim. "And some of us don't." He added as he looked at Judy Blair.

"Hey, Dad," said Jessica, "Some of us are going out, so I won't be home until eleven."

"Okay, kid, but not a second later." Tim warned. She gave him a hug, excused herself and then was gone.

"Nice kid," I said.

"She'll do," Tim answered in a typical Maine understatement.

"Are you going to the class get-together at the New Meadow's Inn?" asked Tim.

"I hadn't planned on it,' I said.

"Come along, I'll buy you a drink. I've heard that Barry Marshall has made a power point presentation of our graduating class's highlights." There was some emotion in Tim's eyes that I couldn't read.

"Sure, how can I pass that up?" I asked.

"Great! I'll meet you there in twenty minutes."

The New Meadow's Inn was an old-fashioned restaurant and function hall that sits on the New Meadow's river just outside of town. The east side of the river was more of a tidal inlet, and I could smell the salt air as I got out of my car. Tim was as good as his word and had a draft beer waiting for me as I entered the function room.

"Hey," he said when he saw me.

"Hey," I answered. That's me, a great conversationalist.

The first thing I noticed as I looked around was that there were more people here than at the dinner. I guess they wanted to skip the traditional part of the evening a get straight to the partying. Tim and I circled the room and whenever he sensed that I didn't recognize someone he would say something like 'You remember so-and-so don't you?' Most people had heard about my digging up a skull in my backyard and wanted more details. The one person I couldn't help but recognize was Jason Goulet. At six foot seven, he was hard to miss. Tim is 6'4 and towers over my mere 6' frame, but Jason dwarfed Tim by his height and his girth.

"Hey Ashworth, how's it hanging?" That was Jason all right, a real classy guy.

"Good evening, Mr. Goulet. How nice to see you again," I said slowly in my upper class mimicking voice.

"Ashworth, you always were an asshole!" he answered, but smiled as he said it. I liked Jason. He was a big guy that never used his size threateningly.

"Hey, I heard Bitch Blair is available. Her husband croaked." I informed him. He always had a crush on her in high school and whenever she could, she led him on.

"Thanks, but I'm quite happy, and I am definitely over her. Now she just needs to get over herself." Jason was no fool.

"Attention everyone! The class slide show is about to begin. Please take your seats," shouted Barry Marshall over the din of the room. Barry had been our class geek well before the age of computers. Now he was setting up an impressive array of computers, projectors, and sound equipment.

Barry darkened the room, and the slide show began. There was 70's rock music playing in the background as text and pictures appeared and dissolved on the screen. These were images of us in our high school days that we hadn't seen for decades. As the images flashed by one image caught my attention and sent a chill down my spine.

"Stop the slides!" I yelled. "Tim, look at that photo!"

"That's Helga Johanson, the foreign exchange student." Tim informed me.

"No, look at what she's wearing, Tim!"

"Oh, my God!" Tim gasped. On the screen was a young blonde Helga Johanson wearing a polyester pink and yellow polka dotted dress. The material looked just like the material that was found with the skull.

Chapter 5

The last week of school went agonizingly slow. Summer in southern New Hampshire can be brutal. It was ninety degrees with ninety percent humidity. The schools are not air-conditioned and the students were sticking to their seats. We had four days of final exams and then Friday was euphemistically called a "teacher workshop" day. In reality we passed in our grades and room keys, and then took a two-hour lunch at a function room with a bar. I had already signed off on the Manchester house, but the new owners were letting me stay on until the last day of school. Argus was spending everyday this week in doggy daycare. I didn't want him left in an empty and stifling house.

I worked on grading the final exams and giving grades for the last time. On Friday I turned in my grades, gave my department head my book inventory and keys, and headed out the door to Tosca's Banquet Room. Those of us who were retiring were seated at one table. It was a bittersweet moment. We had all worked for thirty years or more at Amoskeag High and most of us were taking early retirement. I would miss teaching, but I was looking forward to the changes that were coming. The principal, aka the Amazing Asshole, got up to speak, recognized our years of service, and then it was over, just like that.

I packed up my few belongings at the house and left the keys on the kitchen counter and locked the door behind me. Once outside I walked around the house. The bushes and perennials that I planted some twenty years ago when I bought the house were now lush and mature. I would miss this house; I hope I was doing the right thing by moving on. I picked up Argus at doggy day care, paid the bill, and settled him in the front seat. Argus gave me kisses, circled around in his seat and fell asleep.

I was heading out of Manchester and leaving behind thirty years of my life. As I drove toward the coast I was thinking of Helga Johanson. Helga came to the states from Denmark as a foreign exchange student during our senior year. We didn't know much about her, but she was friendly and outgoing and quickly joined our little social circle. She never talked much about Denmark, other than that she grew up in an orphanage, studied hard, and had always wanted to see America. Two days after graduation she left town to go back to Denmark. At least that's what we thought.

Seeing the photo of her wearing a dress with the same design as the cloth buried with the skeleton had been a shock. Of course it really didn't mean anything. That could have been a popular pattern back in the 70's. Still it was disturbing.

At the class reunion I saw Tim morph from Tim Mallory, high school hero into Police Chief Timothy Mallory. He quickly got Barry Marshall to print out photos of Helga and gave them to the state investigators. Then he pulled her old files from the high school to see what information they might contain. I noticed at the party that most of our classmates were polite to Tim, but that those who still lived in Bath stayed away from him. I wasn't quite sure why.

As I passed over the bridge from New Hampshire into Maine the air seemed to change. I

37

was beginning to relax and was looking forward to starting over. I would wake up in my new life tomorrow morning and not look back; at least that's what I told myself. I would fix up the house, work in the garden, and help out Rhonda at the store. It would be a relaxing summer.

I took the highway to Portland because trying to take the more scenic route one would be too slow during the summer season. I took I-295 through Portland. I love seeing the city skyline and smelling the B&M Baked Bean plant as I headed over Tookey's bridge. Argus liked the smell, too, because he woke up and began sniffing the air. Anything to do with food and he was ready!

The Friday night traffic from Portland to Bath was heavy. I wasn't in a hurry because Rhonda had said that she would pick up a sandwich and some chips and leave them in the house for me. She had a key and was opening the house for the kitchen workers while I was away.

It was still daylight when I pulled into the driveway. Argus woke up and was anxious to get out of the car. The move didn't seem to upset him at all. That's the great thing about dogs. To them the concept of home is a person, not a place. If I was here then Argus was at home. I wasn't sure what 'home' was for me or if I would ever find it. If I clicked my ruby slippers together and chanted, "There's no place like home!" where would I end up?

· · · · · · · · · · · ·

The evening was warm with a slight breeze as I unlocked the front door and stepped inside. I could

Stephen E. Stanley

smell glue and paint, so I suspected that work had progressed on my kitchen. Argus raced around the house sniffing everything in sight. I looked in the kitchen and was surprised by how much work had been done in a week. It had been six months of construction and now the only thing left to do was finish up the kitchen. I took my sandwich and chips, cracked open a beer and went out to the screen porch to eat.

Working with the kitchen people had not been easy. They had tried to sell me on the idea of cherry cabinets, granite counters, and stainless steel appliances. When I suggested that I didn't want to whore up my kitchen to look like a prefab condo they took offense. I had to explain very patiently that such a kitchen was more for show than function, but also that it's unlikely that they had stainless steel appliances in 1925. I told them that I wanted white bead board cabinets, soapstone counters, and a French cook stove built into a tile hearth.

When I went to culinary school for six weeks one summer in France, I fell in love with the big cast iron and enamel gas ranges that French country cooks used. I told the kitchen people that I was interested in function, not status, and they finally agreed that my kitchen design was much better for the space. The big gas range still needed to be hooked up, the refrigerator plugged in, and some cabinet trim finished. It looked like they would be done with the finishing touches in a few days.

After eating I finished unloading the car, I took Argus for a walk, and then fell into bed and was quickly asleep.

A Midcoast Murder

Chapter 6

The sound of a truck backing into the driveway woke me up. There was a loud clatter and I looked out to see three cords of firewood being dumped in the driveway. Later I would stack it in neat piles to season during the summer. I had the fireplace fitted with a wood stove insert so that I could heat with wood on occasion and save on the cost of oil.

I made coffee and dry toast for breakfast, then put Argus in a harness and leash and headed out the door. It was a little over a mile from my house to Rhonda's store on Front Street. We walked down Washington Street past the library to the lower end of Front Street and up the hill to her store. Reny's department store was already open so it was later than I thought. I hadn't bothered to look at the time. I guess retirement wasn't going to be that difficult.

"Hi Guys," greeted Rhonda as we entered the shop. Argus made a run for Rhonda, who quickly gave him a doggy treat, and then he headed to his bed behind the counter to chew on his plastic bone.

"Hi yourself. Thanks for the sandwich, by the way, and also for letting the kitchen people in."

"No problem," answered Rhonda. "You should have seen them trying to get the gas stove through the door! Very entertaining."

"They're almost done. I'll have to have a house warming as soon as it's finished. I'll finally be able to cook."

"Cake!" said Rhonda as she pounded the counter. "I want cake!" It really didn't matter what else I cooked, but Rhonda always loved a piece of cake.

"Okay, Marie Antoinette, I'll look for my chocolate cake recipe," I promised.

"I love the kitchen design, especially the window seat and the bookcase that you had designed for your Maine cookbook collection." I had for years been collecting old cookbooks at yard sales and auction houses. I found some very tasty recipes that I had been able to modernize.

Just then a customer came in. Rhonda took over the shop, and I logged on to the computer to check the online sales. Several orders were there so I packed up the merchandise for a delivery service pick up. About a half hour later we were able to resume our conversation.

"Police Chief Hot Stuff was here pumping me for information about you," Rhonda informed me. I gave her a look.

"I'm sure he thought he was pumping you for information, but I know you, and the reality is that you were the one doing the pumping and the poor bastard didn't even know what hit him," I responded.

"Damn straight!" she laughed.

"So what did he ask?" I wanted to know.

"What other people thought of you, types of things you liked to do, that sort of thing," Rhonda replied.

"Oh, my God!" I exclaimed, "You didn't really tell him did you?"

"What, that a few misguided people love you, but that most people think you are an annoying little prick? Of course not! I did manage to get some information about him. He never clued in that I got the information and he got the questions," she boasted.

"I don't get it," I said, "Why is he asking questions about me?"

"You can be so dumb sometimes!" Rhonda just rolled her eyes and shook her head.

"So," I continued, "What did you learn?" Screw her, I thought.

"Well," she started, "I got the whole scoop. He graduated from Morse High with you, went into the navy, was shipped south and married a Southern girl. He came back and attended the police academy and got a job here. He brought his lovely bride who hated Bath and everyone in it. By the time he found out marriage wasn't for him she was pregnant. She left him after the baby was born and returned south. She married a doctor in Boca and then shipped the kid back to her father. He worked his way up the police ladder. He had to prove himself, so he said he became a complete asshole to win the respect of the town. The result is they think he's a good cop, but they don't really like him."

"Wow! You are good!" I was impressed. Just then a good-looking, middle-aged man walked into the store. Rhonda almost tripped over herself getting out from around the counter. I checked to make sure my work was done and decided to head out.

"Argus," I asked quietly, "You want to go for a walk?" The pug immediately started skipping around. The question was a mere formality. All I really had to say was the word "walk" and he would be bounding around. I put his harness and leash on and headed out the door, giving Rhonda a wave as I went. She was busy chatting up the customer and didn't seem to notice.

We walked to the small park along the Kennebec River. I sat on a bench and Argus jumped on to my lap. I was in no hurry to go back to the house. All the chores that had to be done could wait. It seemed like all I had ahead of me was time. From the bench I could see the traffic whizzing over the new Millennium Bridge. The old Carleton Bridge, rusting beside, it was closed and seemed to remain as a decayed reminder of the past. Maybe my past? Beyond the two bridges was the sound of heavy machinery at the shipyard. They were going full tilt even though it was Saturday. I heard the crunch of gravel as a car pulled into the parking lot.

"Hey, Ashworth! How's it hanging?" It could only be that giant, Jason Goulet.

"Hi Jason. Your keepers let you free for the day?" I asked. Argus greeted him like an old friend. Never trust a guy your dog doesn't like.

"Just barely," he responded. "I've been thinking of Helga. You remember how we were all friends and hung around together? Do you think the bones in your yard were hers?"

"I hope not," I said truthfully. "But I've got a bad feeling about all this." Alas, poor Yorick, I thought to myself.

"Tim Mallory turned over the school records to the state boys. They've been around town asking questions." He reported. "But it was all so long ago, who can remember?"

"It was a long time ago. I didn't even remember her until I saw the slide show. I'm sure I'm on the police interrogation list," I said.

Just then Jason's cell phone rang and after a brief conversation he said, "Got to go. Business is booming and I have to make some money. See you later on I'm sure."

After he was gone I realized I didn't even know what his business was. I had a lot of catching up to do.

"Well," I said to Argus, "I think we have to take that walk down memory lane today." Argus just wagged his curly tail. I had been avoiding my old neighborhood. I wasn't sure what memories, good or bad, the sight of the house where I grew up would evoke. It was time to check it out.

We walked back into town, up Walker Street hill to High Street and passed the high school and then cut over to Middle Street and up the narrow street to Laurel Lane. My parents had sold the house in the early eighties and moved to Florida. The house looked about the same, except that everything was fresher and cleaner. It was an old Cape Cod style house, white with green shutters. The new owners had added a two-car garage and breezeway to the house.

Memories came flooding back. I remembered coming home for lunch when I was in elementary school, playing in the back yard, and sneaking a cigarette behind the shed. But really the emotional impact I expected wasn't there. I missed my parents, but I talked to them every week and went once or twice a year to Florida. They never expressed an interest in coming back to Bath.

"Okay Argus, Let's go home!" Argus was ready and tugged on the leash all the way back to Sagamore Street.

· · · · · · · · · · · · · · · · ·

I was stacking firewood when the state investigators showed up. Argus was tuckered out from all the walking, and he was sleeping on a blanket under a tree and didn't even know anyone was there. Pugs are not watchdogs!

"Hello Mr. Ashworth. I'm Jack Bradley and this is my partner Amanda Gower."

"Hello," I replied cautiously.

"Could you tell us again about finding the skeletal remains?" asked Ms. Gower.

"Sure, have a seat," I indicated the picnic table. I gave them a brief account about digging a vegetable patch and turning up the skull.

"So Jess, did you have any indication that there was anything different about this part of the yard? A depression in the ground? Or maybe a slight mound?" asked Jack Bradley.

'No," I answered. "And the name is Jesse, two syllables. Actually, I chose the spot because it was rather flat and had lots of sun. It was perfect for a little victory garden."

"We have had very little to go on," said Amanda Gower. "We haven't matched the remains up with any missing person files and we've been unable to confirm any link with Helga Johanson Any information you might have would be helpful."

I gave them what little information I had on the house's previous owners, plus all the information I could remember about Helga. They asked a few more questions and then took their leave. I wasn't much help, I guess.

I went back to stacking wood while Argus watched me with one eye open. There was nothing like stacking firewood to give a person time for contemplation. What I like about yard work was that, unlike grading student papers, you could see an immediate improvement.

I was thinking about my high school days and all the times we students spent passing notes back and forth without being caught when a memory hit me! Something so trivial and so insignificant that it might just be the clue needed to break the case.

Chapter 7

It was a beautiful Sunday morning when I woke up, bright sunlight and a cool sea breeze. A little fog was over the river, but it would burn off by mid-morning. I had agreed to go to church with Rhonda, so after coffee, I got dressed, put Argus in his crate, and drove to Rhonda's condo to pick her up.

I found a parking space near the church, and we walked up the steps and into the meetinghouse. I noticed that the Lowells were seated in one of the back pews and Tim and his daughter Jessica were in one of the front pews. I spotted Bill and Becky Simpson across the aisle from us.

I leaned over to Rhonda and whispered, "Does everyone in town go to church here?" I asked.

"Just about," she replied. "They don't call it All Souls Church for nothing."

"I didn't see all these people the last time you dragged me here." I complained.

"I didn't 'drag you here' you insignificant twit, and it was the minister's Away Sunday; she was doing a pulpit exchange with Fist Parish in Portland. Now she's back and the church is packed." I had to admit, for a summer Sunday it was pretty full.

I was about to comment on something when the organ prelude began. The readings this Sunday were from Thoreau's *Walden*. It was one of my favorite books. The minister, Mary Bailey, gave a sermon keeping with the theme of appreciation for the natural world. As both an English teacher and a gardener, I fully appreciated the sermon. So, I guess, did a lot of people because I saw nods of agreement all around.

"See why they all love her?" Rhonda said to me as we filed out. I introduced myself to Mary Bailey on the way out. It was such a beautiful day that coffee hour was being held on the front lawn.

"Great sermon, wasn't it, Jesse?" I turned to find Becky Simpson with her husband Bill in tow.

"I really enjoyed it," I said. I really had, much to my surprise.

"Hey," said a voice behind me. I turned to see Tim Mallory behind me.

"Hey, yourself," I replied. Why do policemen make me tongue-tied? Or was it just this one? "I thought you went to the other church. You know, the one with all the crosses and statues?" That was the best I could do for conversation.

Tim spit on the ground, "Long story," he said.

"Okay then..." there wasn't much for me to say to that. "I remembered something about Helga that may help in the investigation."

"I've been meaning to talk to you about the case. How about if I come over later in the afternoon to your place? Right now I have to go on duty because we are short on staff during vacation time."

"Sure, I should be home later. Stop by," I replied. Tim signaled to his daughter and they both left. Rhonda and I stayed for a while longer at coffee hour and then left for brunch.

We drove south on route one to a restaurant in Freeport famous for its Sunday brunch. The white clapboard inn looked simple and rustic on the outside, but was very elegant on the inside. We sat in a corner and were served by an older waitress who was very attentive. Over steak and eggs we discussed the plan for the week. I would come to the shop on some mornings and help her with the on-line orders. She had hired Brad Watkins, a high school junior, to work in the store, which would help free Rhonda up from having to be in the store all the time. Brad seemed like a nice, capable young man. At 6'2' he seemed much older than seventeen. I would work two or three mornings a week, just enough so I wouldn't be bored. I wasn't sure how my increase in time and decrease in income was going to work.

"You'll be fine," Rhonda assured me. "Look what I did. I left my job of thirty-five years, moved here, where I knew no one, and started a business. And I'm doing great. I even met someone!"

"You did?" I don't know when she had time. "Is it serious?" I asked.

"It will be if I have any say in the matter!" Rhonda was never shy about men. "You remember the guy who came to the shop yesterday morning when you were getting ready to leave?"

"Vaguely," I answered.

"Well, he asked me out!" she said. Before I could ask her any details her cell phone rang. Neither she nor I ever use cell phones casually. She looked confused, fumbled in her purse and took out the phone. "Hello?" she said tentatively. I couldn't hear what was being said on the other end, but Rhonda looked shaken. "Okay," she said and hung up the phone.

"Are you Okay?" I asked.

"No!" she answered, "This is tragic news!" she wailed.

"Oh, no." I'd rarely seen Rhonda this upset. "Did someone die?"

"Much worse than that!" she wailed louder.

"What is it?" I asked. I was getting alarmed.

"My sister is coming to visit!" she cried.

Chapter 8

It was late Sunday afternoon and I was sitting in a rocker on the screen porch in the back of the house. It was a buggy afternoon, and I was grateful for the screens and the slight breeze in the backyard. Argus was sleeping on the floor trying to catch a breeze.

Rhonda had recovered from her phone call and we were able to finish brunch and then do some shopping at L.L.Bean. I had met Rhonda's sister Janice twice before; she was a successful book agent in New York. I thought Janice was a hoot, but Rhonda always felt insecure around her older sister. Janice had been married as many times as Rhonda, but the difference was that each time Janice got rid of a husband, she got richer. Rhonda, on the other hand, never made a dime on her marriages.

Argus heard the car in the gravel driveway before I did and started barking. "Hey, Ashes, are you in there?" It was Tim Mallory rapping on my front screen door.

"Hey Tim," I yelled. "Come on in. I'm on the back porch."

"Hey little fella!" said Tim, though not to me but to Argus, who was beside himself with joy.

"I think you made a friend," I remarked.

"I hope so!" Tim looked up at me and somehow I didn't think he was talking about Argus. Tim straightened up from patting the dog's head and said; "I saw the Eagle's Nest sign when I came in. I didn't notice it before. It sure seems right for this place for some reason."

"The sign was here when I bought it. It seemed right to keep it, though," I replied.

"You've done a great job fixing up the house. It looks great."

"Thanks, they should finish up the kitchen tomorrow and then I'll have all the major appliances," I said.

"Oh, I almost forgot I was holding this." Tim passed me a bottle of chilled white wine. It was a very good brand and a good year.

"Sit down Tim. I'll go get some glasses." I had some glasses somewhere in a box in the kitchen.

"You always liked cooking," Tim remarked as I searched for the glasses. "I always thought you would end up as a chef. Do you remember the trip to Moosehead Lake the three of us took our senior year?"

"Sure," I answered. "It was you and me and Jason Goulet. That was a fun time."

"And," continued Tim, "You astounded us with lunch when we arrived. You popped open the hood of the truck and there were hot dogs and corn-on-the-cob wrapped in tin foil and cooked on the engine."

"Yes," I admitted, "it was a bit of an experiment. It's a wonder they didn't get sucked into the engine fan, or fall off onto the road."

"We ate like kings that weekend and you did all the cooking," Tim said and then quickly changed the subject as I handed him a glass of wine "So you said you remembered something about Helga?" he asked.

"It's nothing really," I replied. "I just remembered something when the state investigators were asking me questions. Helga passed a note to me in study hall once and said she had a tooth that was bothering her. She asked what dentist I used. I remembered the incident because it was one of the few times I got caught passing notes in study hall."

"So?" asked Tim.

"So if she went to the dentist, wouldn't there be dental records? That would at least eliminate or confirm her as the deceased" I responded.

"Shit," swore Tim. "You're right!" Who was your dentist?"

"Dr. Jacobs," I answered.

"The guy's been dead for years," Tim said. "Still, his records must be around somewhere. I'll look into it. Thanks Jesse." Tim held out his glass for a refill. I filled his glass and then topped mine off too.

"Cheers!" I offered.

"Cheers!" answered Tim as we clinked our glasses together.

. . . .

The next day the kitchen crew showed up to finish the kitchen. The propane tanks arrived and the stove was hooked up. I went to the supermarket and shopped, came home and unpacked kitchen boxes, and the house was done. I was fully moved in. I was ready to rock and roll or whatever!

To celebrate my first day in a completed house Argus and I took a nap on the sofa. Argus actually naps most of the time. I, on the other hand, like to nap in the early afternoon. It was a long nap and by the time I woke up it was time to fix dinner.

The kitchen had turned out better than I expected. I reached for a big fry pan from the pot rack and set it on the stove top. I turned the burner on and the gas ring appeared. So far, so good. I tossed in some chicken breasts and browned them. Then I threw in some cut up potatoes, carrots, onions, and a few green beans for color. I added a cup of chicken broth, put on the cover, and simmered it for thirty-five minutes. I was a simple meal, but very good. Tomorrow I would grind up the leftovers and make chicken hash.

It felt great to be able to cook again. I'd been without a fully stocked kitchen for a long time. I loaded up a plate, cracked open a beer and headed to the back porch with Argus trailing in my wake. Yes, I thought to myself, retirement was going to be okay.

By seven o'clock, the heat was gone and I took Argus for a walk. We walked north on High Street. People were out mowing their grass and working in their gardens. Here and there I could see the light of a TV in the window, but in general it was too nice a night to be inside. As we walked up a side street I saw a familiar figure mowing a lawn.

"Hey Goulet," I shouted. "Nice career choice!"

"Ashworth, you always were, you still are, and you will always be a total and complete asshole!" Jason said grinning at me.

"Sticks and stones!" I replied.

"Come on in and have a beer, and bring that ugly dust mop, too," he said pointing to Argus. I followed him into the rather tidy and small 1950's ranch house. We went into the kitchen where he handed me a beer, then we went out to a small deck off the kitchen and sat down.

"Jason, it's been years. I feel out of touch with so much. The town looks the same, but it's like

55

it's been replaced with strangers, or at the very least I feel like Rip van Winkle and I just woke up after years of sleep. I don't even know what you do for work, if you're married, have kids or what." I hadn't meant to blurt out my feelings like that, but I guess I'd had too many changes in so short a time.

"I work as an accountant at the Bath Iron Works. I'm divorced, two grown kids and that's about it. How about you?" asked Jason. "You left after high school and only came back once or twice."

"I went to the University of Southern Maine, got a job teaching high school English in Manchester, New Hampshire, got my masters degree in Vermont, traveled some summers, worked as a cook on a sail boat on several occasion. Got married once, divorced two years later, got my life back, took early retirement, and now I'm here. That's all." Those, at least, were the highlights and the low lights. We chatted for another hour, getting caught up on the local characters we both knew.

"So tell me about Tim Mallory," I asked. "People seem to not like him around here."

"We all like Tim, but he's had a hard time being himself. He is always the cop and doesn't seem to know when to go off duty. Then there is Tracy, the ex-wife. She made it very clear that she hated us. Some people have long memories," Jason explained.

"But nothing specific? He hasn't ticked off anyone or made enemies?" I asked.

"Probably a few criminals here and there. But Bath isn't exactly crime central."

"Well," I looked at my watch, "I should be getting Argus back home." Argus was asleep in my lap and could care less about going home. "I'm going to christen my new kitchen on Sunday evening, if you would like to come."

"Sure, I'd love to Jesse. What time?" Jason asked.

"Six o'clock. I'm only a few blocks away on Sagamore." I wrote down my address and phone number for him. "Okay, Argus, let's go!" Argus was awake and leading me home in no time.

....

The next morning I was up early and baking donut muffins to take to the shop. I found the recipe in an old Maine cookbook and used it to test the new oven. They were easy to make and tasted like molasses doughnuts, without the fat. When they were cool enough I packed them up, put Argus on a leash, and headed to Front Street.

When I entered the shop Brad Watkins was at the counter and Rhonda was the office.

"Good morning Brad," I said and then yelled in Rhonda's direction, "Muffins!" Rhonda came running out of the office, grabbed the bag of muffins, and took a whiff.

"Ashworth, you are a saint! A freaking saint," she exclaimed. "Brad, wait until you taste these! I'll put the coffee on."

I went to the computer and worked on the mail orders. We took a coffee break around ten o'clock. "When is your sister coming?" I asked.

"Saturday, she'll be here for a week. What am I going to do with her?" Rhonda complained.

"Bring her to supper on Sunday night. I'm going to cook, finally"

Just then the door to the shop opened and Tim Mallory stepped in. He nodded at Brad and Rhonda and then turned to me and said, "Jesse, do you have a minute?"

"Sure," I answered. "Rhonda may we use your office?" I sure was seeing Tim pop up a lot in my life lately.

"Of course you may. Tim, would you like some coffee? And Jesse just baked some muffins. Take one," she offered.

Tim declined the coffee, but took the offered muffin. "These are great!" he said with his mouthful.

"Thanks, Tim," I said. "So what's happening?"

"I've got a guy looking for Dr. Jacob's old records."

"Well, I hope he finds them," I offered.

"Me, too. I really could use your help on this case, Jesse."

"Really? What could I do?" I asked.

"If I start asking questions, people will just clam up and not talk. They'll be very guarded in what they say. You, on the other hand, can ask all types of questions without raising suspicions. And even if you do seem a little nosy, it was your backyard that the remains were found. It would make sense that you were asking questions."

"Sure, I'll do it!" It would be like being a detective, and besides I was retired and wouldn't be that busy.

"Great, let's get together later and look over the case," Tim suggested.

"Stop by when you get off duty," I said.

. . . .

It was a very warm afternoon and the air was scented with blossoms of various types. The bees were busy in the garden and, despite the short growing season in Maine, all my plantings were doing well. Argus had found a cool spot on the floor and was watching me puttering around the house. It was a bad year for pollen, and I had to dust off the green pollen every day, just to keep pace with it.

I was in the kitchen going through my Maine cookbooks, looking for recipes when I heard Tim drive up in his pickup truck. Argus made a beeline to the door to greet him.

"Come on in!" I called through the screen door.

"Beautiful afternoon out there!" he said by way of a greeting. I think Mainers talk about weather more than any other topic. It must be a holdover from the farming and fishing days when weather conditions were a matter of life and death.

"Plan on staying for supper," I said. "Unless, of course, you have other plans." In Maine we still use the term supper for the evening meal.

"Free as a bird. Jessica just left for the airport to fly down to visit her mother for the summer. She'll be back in the fall to start college at Orono," Tim informed me.

"Beer or wine?" I asked.

"Wine."

"Red or white?"

"White!"

I went into the kitchen to grab a bottle of wine. Tim followed me in.

"Wow!" Tim exclaimed. "This is some kitchen. It's as cozy as my grandmother's and yet looks like a place for some serious cooking."

"Do you cook?" I asked

"Yes, I had to learn when I became a single parent. Just the basics, plus lots of takeout. Jessica has been helping with the cooking. She really is a good kid," Tim explained.

"Which, I'm sure," I added, "means that you are a good parent. By the way, I'm having a house warming on Sunday, so plan on coming for supper." I handed him a glass of wine. My plan to have 'a few people over' seemed to expanding into a party.

"I will be there," he said. He sat down at the kitchen table. "Here's a list of the people I'd like you to talk to." The list included the Lowell's because they lived next door during the time when they think the body was buried. Jason Goulet, as well as Bill and Becky Simpson, Judy Blair, and Sue Abbot were on the list because we all knew her in high school.

"Not Bitch Blair!" I complained. "I have to talk to her?"

"Yup," replied Tim. "Better you than me. I think she wants to get reacquainted with me, and I want nothing to do with her."

"She always had the hots for you," I teased.

"Yes, well today we would call her a stalker. Back then we thought she was just a nut job."

I came up with an idea. "I think I'll invite everyone here on Sunday. Some food and wine might jog some memories and loosen some tongues. I'm not having Bitch Blair in this house, though."

"Good idea," Tim replied. "On both counts."

Tim and I chatted while I made supper. I took the leftover one-pot chicken dinner from yesterday, ran it through the food processor, and put it in a hot fry pan. I made some corn meal biscuits and put them in the oven. I opened a jar of pickle beets. Argus was under my feet hoping some food would fall his way. Before long, supper was ready.

"Wow Ashworth," exclaimed Tim, "You've still got it in the kitchen department. This is very good."

"Not to mention," I added, "very cheap and simple to prepare."

"What's for dessert?" asked Tim.

"Rhubarb pie," I said.

"Oh my God! That's my favorite!"

"I know," I said. "I can't remember where I was yesterday, but I can remember that you liked rhubarb pie from decades ago." Memory is the first casualty of aging. Or maybe it was the second; I don't really remember. After dessert we went into the living room for coffee.

"So here is what we know so far," he began. "We have the remains of a young woman, buried in your backyard sometime between 1970 and 1975, cause of death unknown. There is a medallion with a date 1969 which may or may not be related to the death. We have the remnants of some clothing. We have a photograph of Helga Johanson wearing a dress made of a very similar cloth. We have no confirmation from Denmark that Helga is or is not alive. And we have a two-person team of state investigators from Augusta who seem not to be that interested in finding answers."

"We'll have more to go on once we find out if it is Helga or not," I said. "That is if we can locate old Dr. Jacob's records."

Just then Tim's cell phone went off.

"Shit," he said after he hung up. "I have to go. One of the officers went home sick."

"It's always something, isn't it? I asked.

"It sure is!" he muttered as he was going out the door.

After Tim left, Argus and I stretched out on the sofa. When I first began to tell people I was retiring they all asked, "What are you going to do?" I was getting very tired of the question as if a person always has to have something to do. I finally answered by saying "I'm going to lounge on my sofa and gaze at all my stuff." That was exactly what I was doing now, gazing at all my stuff. Argus was curled up next to me, and it wasn't long before I fell asleep. I had weird dreams and in the dreams I was running around searching for something. I looked everywhere and I began digging up my back yard. I was digging deeper and deeper and then finally I unearthed something. It was a computer. Just as I was brushing off the dirt I woke up with a start. It was close to midnight and I said to Argus, "I have an idea! I know where to find some of the answers." I was excited, but Argus could have cared less.

Chapter 9

Morning came, and with it were the sounds of summer. Anyone who thinks that Maine is a peaceful and quiet place probably has never been here. Each season has its own sounds. In winter there is the thunderous cracking of the ice on the rivers and lakes; in spring we have the spring peepers that sing as night begins to settle; in summer we have the buzzing of the cicadas as the day heats up; in late summer the crickets fill the night air with sound, and in the fall there is the honking of the geese as they seek warmer climes. In all seasons we have the wind and the sea. On this late June morning the birds were raising a ruckus. Far from singing, this morning the sounds were of avian war.

I set my notebook computer on the kitchen table and sat down with a cup of coffee. Dr. Jacobs had been a medic during World War II and had married late in life. Ben, his only child was two years behind my graduating class. Since both parents were dead and he had no siblings, he could be anywhere. First I emailed the Morse High Alumni office to see if they had an address for Ben. I wasn't sure how often the office would be staffed so I decided to try an Internet search by entering the name Benjamin Jacobs in a search engine to see what came up.

Apparently this wa a named shared by various famous and not so famous persons. I was able to eliminate lots of the entries right away. I found two dentists with that name and thought maybe he had followed his father's profession, but when I went to the dental practices web pages the one dentist was too young and the other one was too old. Dead end! Just as I was about to give up a chime informed me that I had mail. It was from the alumni office, but I was disappointed when I read it. The last address they had for Ben was from 1980 when he was in law school.

Argus was getting restless, which was a sign that I should take him for a walk. I put his harness on and we headed up the street. Next door, Dorothy Lowell was out tending her flowers.

"Good morning Mrs. Lowell," I said by way of greeting.

"Good morning, Jesse," she responded. "Call me Dorothy. I'm not your third grade teacher anymore. In fact, now that you've retired, we are in the same club, so to speak." She laughed at that. "Beautiful morning isn't it?"

"It certainly is. I'm having a few people over on Sunday night for supper and I'd like you and John to come," I said.

"What can I bring?" she asked. A Maine housewife of her generation would never think of going visiting without bringing something. Still, it was correct for me to protest.

"Just bring yourselves," I assured her. I knew full well she would bring some goodies with her.

Just then Argus decided to take a giant poop on her lawn. I leaned over and picked it up with a plastic baggie. Time to go!

"Okay," I added as we headed back home. "See you Sunday, around six o'clock."

I decided to check the Internet again and try a Boolean search using Ben Jacobs' name and the word "attorney." This time I hit the jackpot. I found an attorney in Brookline, Massachusetts, with the same name. There was a picture of him on the law office's website. Bull's eye! I picked up the phone and dialed the number.

"Good morning," I greeted the receptionist. "I'm from the Morse High School Alumni Association in Bath, Maine," I lied. "We are looking for one of our classmates. Would you happen to know if Ben Jacobs is the same Ben Jacobs who graduated with us?"

I was put on hold; a short time later Ben himself, picked up the call.

"Hello, this is Ben."

"Good morning Ben. You probably don't remember me," I began. "My name is Jesse Ashworth, and I was two years ahead of you at Morse High."

"Actually, Jesse, I do remember you," he paused. "You stood up for me once when a group of bigots called me Jew boy."

"I did?" I didn't remember that.

"Yes, and I owe you one," he prompted.

"Okay, then. Maybe you can help me." I went on to tell him about the bones in my backyard and the possibility of his father's dental records being helpful.

"I have a storage locker for my older legal files. When my father died, I had his records moved there. I haven't had time to dispose of them yet, so if Helga was a patient of my father's they would be there."

I thanked him and told him I'd let the investigators know where to look.

"Okay, Argus," I said to the dog. "Let's go visit the police station."

The police department had grown quite a lot since I was in high school. Back then the office was located in the basement of city hall. Now it was located in a new building on Water Street. The department had grown to twenty-six full time employees. As I entered an officer looked up from behind a glass partition.

"Yes, can I help you?" she asked.

"I'm here to see Chief Mallory," I explained.

Before she could respond Tim stepped out of his office and saw me.

"Hey, Jesse, what are you doing here?" he asked.

I told him about tracking down the dental records. I thought he would be pleased, but he looked like he could spit nails.

"How long did it take you to do this, Jesse?" he asked, keeping his voice even.

"Probably about an hour," I said. Was I in trouble?

"Really!" he replied. Then he leaned over to the office at the desk. "Get detective O'Brien out here, now"

A plain-clothes officer, whom I took to be O'Brien, appeared shortly.

"What's up chief?" he asked.

"How's the search for the Johanson dental records going?" he asked O'Brien.

"Kind of slow, if you know what I mean. The doctor being dead and all makes it hard to get any information," reported O'Brien.

"Really?" Tim asked, his voice changing suddenly. "Because," he said to O'Brien with a look of amusement, "Mr. Ashworth here tracked them down in about an hour. One more slip up like this and I'm busting you down to parking enforcement and to hell with the union! Now stay out of my way!"

O'Brien paled visibly and left the room very quickly. As soon as he was out of sight, Tim smiled.

"I've wanted a reason to nail his ass to the wall for some time. Thanks for giving me a reason." Tim said happily. "I think tomorrow I'll take a cruiser and go check out the records. Want to come along?" He asked.

"Road trip!" I said by way of an answer.

"Road trip!" Tim echoed.

The rest of the afternoon Argus and I spent at Erebus with Rhonda. Brad had the day off, so it was just the two of us. We got to talk between customers. Today, for some reason, we were talking about teaching and the horror stories of our first year experiences.

"I'd be in teacher jail today," I said thinking about all the litigious events of my career.

"Me too," she said. Things seemed much easier back then.

At six o'clock Rhonda closed up the shop and suggested we go out to eat.

"I can't take Argus into a restaurant, even though he's cleaner and quieter than some people's kids," I said.

"We'll go to Ruby's. They have an outside seating section where you can take Argus," she suggested.

"Perfect," I answered. Ruby's had very good food, a great selection of beer, and outside seating with a view of the river.

We settled for a table in the corner of the patio where we could watch all the comings and goings around us and still have a view of the water. The waitress brought us water and menus. Argus was sitting at my feet looking around.

"Nice selection," I said.

"Simple food the way you like it."

When the waitress returned Rhonda ordered broiled haddock, and I ordered broiled scallops.

"So," I began. "How's your love life? You never got to finish telling me about your date."

"His name is Jackson Bennett, and we are going out for lunch tomorrow. I'll let you know how that goes," Rhonda replied. "And how is your love life?"

"Nonexistent! Who needs a burned out fifty-something, retired school teacher?" I asked.

"Let's see, you work out at least three times a week. You haven't gained a pound in twenty years. You take care of yourself, and you are sharper than a tack, not to mention that you are a hunk. Except that when it comes to realizing that other people actually like you, then you are dumber than warm shit!"

Rhonda was just about to say something else when we both saw Tim Mallory and Sue Abbot walk into the dining room. They didn't see us in the corner as they passed through the patio into the dining room.

"I wondered if Tim was dating anyone. I'm sure someone that good looking isn't too lonely," I said to Rhonda.

"They didn't look all that cozy to me," she replied.

"They were all dressed up and chatting. Looks like a date to me," I said.

Rhonda gave me the eye roll just as our food arrived. The food was so good we ate in silence.

"Do you want to bring Jackson with you when you come over Sunday?" I asked.

"I don't think so. It's too early to introduce him to you," she replied with a wink.

The waitress came by with a dessert tray. It was more effective than a menu. I very rarely have room for dessert, but the treats on the tray were too tempting.

"Honey," Rhonda addressed the waitress. "You just leave that tray right here and come back in ten minutes for the crumbs."

"But..." the waitress stammered.

"She's kidding," I told the waitress. "You know how old ladies are." Rhonda kicked me under the table. "I'll have the chocolate cake."

"Me, too," chimed in Rhonda.

"Would you like ice cream on it?" asked the waitress.

"Does a bear shit in the woods?" asked Rhonda.

"She means yes," I translated to the very confused waitress who scurried away as quickly as she could.

"You are a very evil woman!" I told Rhonda. She just smiled.

As we were leaving the restaurant with Argus in tow, we passed by a window. I could see Tim and Sue sitting at a table chatting it up on their date. Good for you I thought with a sigh.

Tim picked me up in his cruiser around eight the next morning. I had never been in a cruiser before, which I guess is a good thing, and I was duly impressed with the electronics. We stopped briefly in Portland for breakfast and then took the turnpike south toward Boston. We had an easy ride through Boston as people tended to get out of the way of a police car.

"Put on the lights and siren, Tim," I begged.

"No way," He said. Then the siren went off for two seconds. "Oops, hit the wrong button," he said with a smile.

"Cool," I said.

We used a GPS to find Ben Jacobs office. We picked him up and he went with us to the records warehouse in South Boston. I never knew there were such places. Ben showed his ID to the security people and we were let into a small room with shelves.

"Dad's records are over here," he said indicating several boxes on the floor.

"Okay," I said. "They look like they are well-organized." I found the boxes for the appropriate years and alphabetical listings. "Of course this could be a wild goose chase. She may not have gone to the dentist at all."

"Here, let me look." Tim picked up a group of files. "I've done this before, so I know what I'm looking for."

"Good because I don't know where to start," I replied. Ben looked uncomfortable leaning against the wall. "Something wrong, Ben?"

"I could swear that these have been moved. I'm sure I placed them in much neater piles than this. I'm a bit obsessive-compulsive, and I would never leave them in disarray like this."

"Really," asked Tim. "Are you sure?"

"Oh, yes," replied Ben. "I'm very sure now."

"Eureka," cried Tim as he held up a file. He carefully opened it to discover that it was empty.

"Shit," was the only response I could think of.

Ben looked confused and went to another box and pulled out a notebook with plastic sleeves inside.

"Dad didn't want to pay for storage or store all these files in his house. He was in the process of having them digitized when he died." He handed Tim the notebook. The plastic sleeves were holders for CD-ROM's. "I'm not sure how far back the records go, but you can have them."

Tim wrote out a receipt for the CD's and gave it to Ben. On the way out he flashed his badge at an elderly security officer.

"I want to know who has been in to see the Hartman and Jacobs' files," Tim said naming Ben's law firm.

"Let me look," replied the security guard. A few minutes he supplied the information. "A Rita Toliver from Hartman and Jacobs came in last Tuesday."

Tim and I looked at Ben.

"There's no Rita Toliver in my office," protested Ben.

"I was afraid of that," Tim said.

"She must have had identification if we let her in," protested the guard. "We are not a high security facility here. We store old records and most

71

of the information is useless to anyone except our clients."

"Were you working Tuesday?" asked Tim of the guard.

"Yes, I was"

"Do you remember her at all?"

The guard thought for a moment. "No, I guess I don't," he replied.

Tim just sighed.

Ben took us to lunch at Vinnie Testa's. I ate way too much, which is why I have to spend so much time walking and working out. Over lunch the three of us tried to brainstorm ideas on who Rita Toliver was or what the missing records meant, if anything.

"This is going to drive me crazy," Tim sighed. "I hate not getting answers."

"If I hadn't bought the house," I began. "I wouldn't have dug up the skull, and we wouldn't have this problem."

"Well, now my security has been breached," Ben complained.

Ben paid the bill when it came. We thanked him for all his trouble and then we got in the cruiser and headed back to Maine. We tried not to think about the mystery at all and instead talked about places we had been and things we did in the past. It seemed like we were back in Bath in no time. Tim dropped me off at my house.

"I'll have one of my computer geeks check out the CD's. I'll talk to you later," he said as I stepped out. Tim waved as he sped away.

I went into the house and let Argus out of his crate and into the backyard so he could do his business. The backyard looked great, but there was still some bad energy here from the digging up of the remains. I would have to do something about that.

The phone was ringing as I stepped into the house.

"Hello," I said into the phone.

"She's driving me crazy," screeched a hysterical voice, followed by a string of curses. I deduced that Rhonda's sister had arrived and things were not going well. I listened for about five minutes and had about enough.

"Tits to the wind, honey! Suck it up!" I said and hung up. Some people have real problems!

Chapter 10

I was still having some problems feeling displaced. I would wake up in the morning and for a few seconds not know where I was. This bedroom looked much different from my previous house, and I was feeling a bit disoriented. The feeling of being 'at home' was still eluding me. I took Argus out, fed him, and then hopped into the shower while the coffee was brewing. It was already warm, and I knew it was going to be a hot day. I made a pan of blueberry muffins, packed them up, harnessed up Argus, and headed out to Rhonda's shop. I was sure I'd get an earful when I got there, but I knew she couldn't resist a bag of blueberry muffins.

"You hung up on me, asshole!" was the greeting I received when I entered Erebus.

"You were hysterical," I replied. Then I handed her the bag of muffins.

"Maybe I over reacted just a bit," she said with a mouth full of muffin.

"You think?" I asked.

"Good morning," I said as Brad Watkins entered the shop.

"Good morning, Mr. Ashworth," he said as I offered him a muffin. "These are really good."

"Thanks, well I should get on the computer and get to work," I said as I left them to go into the back office. Argus followed me and curled up under the desk.

About midmorning the phone rang, "Erebus" I said into the receiver.

"Hey, Jesse, it's Tim. Can you come over to the office?"

"Sure, I'll be right over."

Stephen E. Stanley

The police department was full of officers coming and going. Several of them stopped to play with Argus. He was in heaven. Any attention was welcome as far as he was concerned.

"What's up?" I asked Tim when he came out of his office.

"My computer whiz, officer Murphy, is coming on duty and I'm going to give her the CD's to see if it will be any help at all."

Officer Jan Murphy was about twenty-five with long blonde hair, and a great figure. Tim introduced us. No wonder Tim liked his job.

"Good morning Mr. Ashworth. The chief has told me all about you." He had? I wondered what that meant. "Hopefully," she continued, "we can find a program that will open these files and see what we've got."

She inserted the CD into the computer and her fingers flew over the keyboard. "This will take a few minutes. I need to download a file reader from the Internet, but I think I'll be able to tell something then."

Tim offered me a cup of coffee, and he and I sat back while Jan worked on the computer. She ejected the first CD and inserted the second. After a few minutes she removed it and put in the third CD. "This is the last one," she said.

"Oh, well. I was hoping we might learn something…" I started to say.

"Wait!" officer Murphy cried. "I think … yes here it is!"

"Good work!" said Tim. "Print out a copy and then send the file to the state medical examiner."

"Will do chief," she said and then hit a series of keys.

"Buy you lunch?" Tim asked me.

"Sure," I replied. "Just let me drop off Argus at the shop. I'm sure Brad wouldn't mind watching him. He's offered before."

The week rolled into Sunday very quickly. We hadn't heard anything from the medical examiner, but we knew it could take a week or longer. I walked through the house straightening up as best I could before people started to arrive. It still felt like I was living in someone else's house, like they could come in at any minute and kick me out. I had transitioned out of the old house okay, but the new house felt strange. All the furniture was new. I only had a few pieces of art that were familiar.

Sunday morning had threatened to be rainy, but the wind came in from the west and cleared away the clouds. The air was much dryer, and it promised to be a very comfortable day.

I put Argus in his crate and went to church. I sat with Rhonda and her sister Janice. I didn't see any signs of violence, so they must be co-existing peacefully for now. Tim came in and sat with us. I was beginning to recognize more people by sight. Pastor Mary Bailey's sermon was about the interdependent nature of community. I wasn't sure I felt like a community member yet, but at least I felt comfortable sitting with Rhonda and Tim. And I knew Tim could break up a fistfight between Rhonda and her sister if need be.

The afternoon I spent in the kitchen. I like to get as much cooking preparation done as possible before the guests arrive. I also like to cook in stages and clean up as I go. The cooks who dirty every pan in the kitchen and then leave the cleanup until after the meal always horrify me. I did much of my cooking for small groups in a ship's galley, and when room is a premium, you have to clean up as you go.

Given the choice between gourmet cuisine and comfort food, I'll go with comfort food every time. Tonight's menu was good food, simply prepared. I had planned individual meatloaves, cornbread, scalloped potatoes, and carrot ring with fresh peas in the center, and chocolate cake for dessert. At the moment I was making gravy for the meatloaf. The secret ingredient was cola, which gives it just enough sweetness and tang to capture attention.

I was uncorking the wine when people began arriving. Jason Goulet was the first to arrive followed by Bill and Becky Simpson. The Lowells walked over from next door; Dorothy, as I suspected, brought along a batch of molasses cookies. Tim Mallory arrived with Sue Abbot. Argus was running around trying to greet everybody and sucking up lots of attention. The last to arrive was Rhonda and her sister Janice. I made introductions, filled wine glasses, put out some crackers and cheese, and then slipped back into the kitchen.

I was planning on making the rounds and asking questions about Helga. I wasn't sure how I could get people alone to ask questions with so many people around, but I could give it a try.

"Need any help?" asked Sue Abbot as she stepped into the kitchen.

A Midcoast Murder

"Not really," I said. "I've got two ovens going and everything should be ready soon."

"This is a really nice kitchen, Jesse."

"Thanks," I replied. Then I blurted out "So you and Tim…"

"We've been good friends for years," she said with a confused look. "We have a lot in common."

"Cool for you," I said a little too sharply. I decided to change my direction a little. "You know," I began with a tone meant to garner sympathy, "this whole idea that the bones I found might be Helga is very upsetting. Do you remember much about her? I'm having a hard time remembering anything significant."

"Not much," Sue answered. "We all liked her. She was very pretty in that blonde Scandinavian way and had that adorable accent. Some of the girls didn't like her. Jealous I expect."

"Who didn't like her?" I asked. "I thought she got along with everyone."

"Judy Blair hated her, but then Judy hated anyone who wasn't wearing pants."

"Do you remember the day she left town?" I asked.

"No, I had already left for my summer job at Old Orchard Beach," she answered.

"Hey, what's up?" It was Becky Simpson.

"We were just talking about Helga Johanson," replied Sue.

"She was a whore!" Becky spit the words rather than said them. We both looked at her.

"Why do you say that?" I asked. The timer went off and I took the corn bread out of the oven to cool.

"She flirted with all the boys and made a spectacle of herself."

"Hey, when do we eat?" It was Jason Goulet leaning in from the living room pass through.

"In about five minutes. Refill everyone's wine glass and get them all in here," I told him.

The food was ready and I lined everything up buffet style on the kitchen counter. Having no formal dining room was fine with me as the dining nook in the kitchen seemed more intimate. I had to put two extra leaves in the table to seat everyone, but there was more than enough room.

When we were all seated the conversation became very lively as everyone dug into the food. Argus took up residence under the table, watching for crumbs and scraps.

"Jesse," Janice addressed me, "this is some of the best home cooking I've ever had." Everybody nodded in agreement.

"Thanks," I replied. One can never have enough compliments, even if they are only being polite.

"Jesse collects old recipes and updates them. He has hundreds of good, simple old fashion recipes that he's worked on," Rhonda said to the table.

"Really?" responded Janice. "I'm a book agent, and I always have publishers looking for cookbooks with a new slant."

"There must be hundreds of cookbooks out there," I replied.

"And there are thousands of readers. Ever since the Food Channel has been on the air, people are interested in cooking again," Janice said. "I'll send you a copy of the manuscript standards. I think you really should write one on comfort food."

"Do it, Jesse!" Tim encouraged.

"Yes, do it, Jesse," said the group.

"We'll see," I said. I wasn't sure if Janice was pulling my leg or not.

"That must have been an awful shock finding a skull when you were digging up a garden," said Dorothy Lowell out of the blue. Talk about a show stopper! I decided to take advantage of the shift in conversation.

"Who was living here then?" I asked Dorothy and John. The Lowell's had lived in the house next door since they were married fifty years ago.

"A family named Nelson owned the house. He was at the Brunswick Naval Air Station and got transferred to Virginia. They rented out the house for several years," answered John.

"There was a group of hippies here in the 1970's," supplied Dorothy. "It was like one of those communes. People were coming and going. Lots of local teenagers were stopping by."

"I think there were drugs here," said John to the table.

"Most likely," said Sue Abbot. "Kids were doing drugs when we were in high school. Weren't they Jason?"

"They were?" asked Jason innocently. Jason was known to try anything back in those days.

"Let's go into the living room for coffee and cake," I said.

"So Tim," said Sue Abbot when we were all settled and coffee and cake were served, "what's going on with the case anyway?"

"I'm afraid it's been too many years. If we don't get a break in the case it's going to be a cold case file," he answered. There was a pause in the conversation as everyone began eating cake.

"Jesse, are you going to show us around?" asked Janice when we had finished out cake.

"Sure, let me stack the dishes and I'll give you the tour. I put the dishes in the dishwasher and set the timer for later.

"Okay, you've seen the living room and the kitchen. There are two bedrooms and the gardens and that's about it." I took them around and showed them the bedrooms. Then we went out to the front porch and I pointed out the name Eagle's Nest on the top of the door.

"Why do you think they named it that?" asked Jason.

"I've no idea," I answered honestly.

"I have an idea," said John Lowell. "I remember Don Nelson telling me about the name when he bought the place in the early 1950's. He bought it from the original owner, who had served in World War I as a pilot. The eagle was some sort of aviation military symbol, but I can't remember what it stood for exactly."

"Well," said Rhonda. "Whatever the story is, it seems to fit this house. And the house seems to fit you, Jesse."

I wasn't so sure about that. I took them around the yard and showed them all the perennials I had planted. Many of the plants were in bloom and very colorful. I had to admit that the yard had turned out well for all its newness.

"And this is where I was going to put a vegetable garden when I found..." and I hesitated, but everyone know what I meant. "I just couldn't finish the garden. Maybe next year I'll try to grow some. I threw some wildflower seeds in the ground here and you can see where some of them are coming up."

There was silence for a few moments.

"Well," announced Jason. "I really need to get going. Tomorrow is a workday for some of us!" he added.

As happens once someone leaves, everyone else follows. Tim offered to stay behind and help me clean up.

Everyone politely thanked me for dinner, and I thanked everyone for coming.

"Did you learn anything tonight?" asked Tim when we were alone.

"The only thing I learned is that I have to ask more questions. Becky Simpson had a violent reaction to Helga's name when I brought it up. I need to get Bill alone without Becky and ask him about it."

"If he is ever alone without her," added Tim.

"And Sue Abbot said that Judy Blair hated her. That means I really have to go see her I guess."

"Good luck with that!" Tim responded. "I'm glad Sue was helpful."

"She was very helpful. How long have you two been dating? I asked.

"Dating? What makes you think that I'm dating Sue Abbot?" Tim's voice was rising.

"I saw you two sitting in the corner at Ruby's the other night. And you were sort of cozy together tonight, too."

"You think I am dating Sue Abbot?" Tim stepped closer to me with his eyes flashing. "Dating Sue Abbot?" he was very close to me now. "I'm friends with Sue Abbot because she lives in Portland and sees me as a friend and not just a cop!" Tim had grabbed hold of me and was pressing me gently against the wall. "Sue Abbot is a lesbian and has been with her partner for twenty years! And you would probably know that if you had stuck around here instead of running off to New Hampshire." Tim was staring at me.

'I didn't run to New Hampshire" I protested. "I drove there!"

"I've had just about enough of you, Ashworth!" Tim said. "You may have college degrees up the ass, but you're sometimes thicker than shit!"

Never piss off a cop!

. . . .

I woke up in the morning to the sound of rain. It sounded like a heavy summer downpour. It took me some time to come out of a very deep sleep. I had a moment of disorientation when I looked out the window and saw sunlight streaming in. It was the shower! Oh my God! I went to sleep and left the shower running!

Just then my memory returned and a very wet and naked Tim Mallory stepped out of the shower.

"You're out of uniform," I said.

"Is that a problem?" he asked with a smile.

I took a closer look. "No, it is definitely not a problem!"

"Good, now get your lazy butt out of bed," Tim laughed as he dried off.

"I'll get up and get the coffee going," I said.

"Already done," he said smiling.

Tim may not be perfect, but from this angle he certainly looked it.

"I have some pancakes I made up ahead and put in the freezer. I can get them ready in about two minutes.

"Perfect," Tim replied.

After breakfast Tim left to go home and change and then go in to work. I wasn't working at Erebus today, so for the rest of the morning I puttered around the house cleaning up after the party. I still had a few boxes in the garage to unpack, the last of some books I brought along and couldn't part with. I figured I better rescue them before they mildewed or got moldy. I carried the box to the front porch and carefully unpacked it, dusting them off as I went. At the bottom of the box was my high school yearbook. I hadn't looked at it in years.

We were named the shipbuilders, I remembered as I flipped through the pages. The words to "The Blue and the White," our school song, were in the opening pages. I had forgotten all about it. I looked though the senior section. How young we all looked! There I was, and Tim, and Jason in jackets and ties. The girls wore blouses with Peter Pan collars. I always wondered how those collars got that name.

In the sports section I found a picture of Jason and me in our Morse High band uniforms. Tim was featured on the football, basketball, and track teams. Bitch Blair and Sue Abbot were on the cheerleading squad with Rebecka Todd, a.k.a. Becky Simpson. Helga Johanson, as one of two foreign exchange students, had a whole page to herself. On the opposite page was Nancy Ramirez from Brazil. I really didn't remember her that well; she took classes with the junior class.

The last section of the yearbook contained pages of candid photos of our class doing various things. Several of them were taken at The Bridge. The Bridge was a coffee shop and hangout that had been opened to give us a place to go. It was the height of the Vietnam War and America was torn apart by politics and division. People were concerned about us as a generation torn apart. The hangout was in the basement of a building that had once been the bottom floor of J.J Newbury's Five and Ten Cent Store. Big wooden wire spools served as tables and were complimented by folding metal chairs. There, in the dim light of The Bridge, was a photo of Helga, Tim, Jason, Judy, Sue and me. The bright flash of an early Instamatic camera illuminated us. Then I saw it! I stared at the photo in disbelief for a few moments, and then I picked up the phone.

Chapter 11

Moxie is the official soft drink of the state of Maine. Anyone not familiar with it might, by looking at the can, mistake it for a regular soft drink. It's not. It has a bitter kick that some people like and some don't. Moxie was invented in 1876 by a doctor from Union, Maine and sold as a medicine. It was said to be a cure for softening of the brain and an enhancement of manhood. No wonder I liked it! I had a supply of it in my refrigerator.

I was sipping on a Moxie wondering what to do next. I had called Tim to tell him about what I saw in the yearbook photograph, but he was out of the office, and I didn't want to leave a message. I flipped open my laptop, did a search, picked up the phone and punched in some numbers.

"Good morning," I said into the receiver, "could I speak to Ms. Blair?" I waited on hold for a few seconds before she picked up. "Hi Judy, it's Jesse Ashworth. Are you free for lunch? I have to drive into Portland for a late afternoon appointment." Lying was getting easier.

"I didn't think I was your type!"

"It's lunch, Judy, not a marriage proposal!" You bitch, I added silently.

"Okay, as long as you're paying. You know where my office is?" she asked.

"Not really," I replied. I jotted down the address. "It should be easy to find."

"What time will you be here?" she asked.

"Around noon."

"I'll see you then," and then she hung up. Charming!

I began to get ready to go, and Argus, from long experience, knew I was going out, and he headed to his crate. Pugs need to be crated when they are left alone, not because they are destructive, but because they are curious and get in lots of trouble when left alone. It's a safety issue. Still, I never leave him in a crate for more than a few hours.

I backed out of the driveway and headed up route one to Portland. It was about a forty-minute drive on a good day. I took the Baxter Boulevard exit and then headed north on Forest Avenue. I found her office easy enough. The sign on the door said Judy Blair Associates, and then in small letters, Beauty Supplies. I enter the office and I could smell the shampoo. I was looking at the shampoo samples when Judy came in.

"Hi, Jesse, looking for some shampoo for thinning hair?" she asked.

"Sure," I replied. "What brand are you using?"

"Smart guy! Where do you want to eat? There's a nice bistro around the corner."

"That would be great." And much faster, too, I thought to myself. The less time I have to spend with her the better.

We walked around the corner to the bistro and sat outside under an umbrella. The waiter brought us water and menus.

"Nice selection," I said.

"The food is good here," she replied.

Judy ordered pot roast with roasted potatoes, green beans, and asked for extra bread.

"I'll have the grilled chicken Caesar salad," I told the waiter and then added: "I'm watching my weight." I can be a bitch, too! We both asked for ice tea. I took a moment to check my cell phone while Judy routed around in her purse for her lipstick. I called home and punched in my answer machine code. No messages. Judy was watching me.

"So," Judy began as she sipped her ice tea, "why are you here? Not that I'm not glad to see you, Jesse."

"I just thought I'd catch up. Also, I'm a little bit upset with the finding of a body and all in my back yard. I'm hoping it's not going to be Helga Johanson What do you remember about her?"

"Well, I've been thinking a lot about it since your theatrical display at the reunion party. I was always one to follow fashion, and I remember that dress. It was ugly and striking, and I never saw that fabric anywhere except for that dress of hers. I don't remember events well, but I can tell you what was in fashion and what was not, and that dress," she emphasized by tapping the table, "was not!"

"I see," I said. "But what did you think of her?"

"The foreign orphan story got old real fast. She used it to get attention and sympathy from the boys especially. She made a play for Tim Mallory when we were going out, and I had to put her in her place. Billy Simpson was always mooning over her, and Jason Goulet, too."

"Never," I protested. "Jason adored you." Bull shit, bull shit, bull shit, I thought as I was saying it. But she looked pleased. I had to suck up until I got all the information I needed.

"Tim Mallory is still a hunk. Do you know if he's going out with anyone? I wouldn't mind renewing that acquaintance," she practically gushed.

"I'll ask around and see what I can do," I promised. When pigs fly, I thought.

"That's cool," she said.

"Did you ever visit the hippies on Sagamore Street back in high school?" I asked just to get back on the subject.

"Sure, several times. Oh," she looked like she just had an original thought. "Was that your house?"

"Yes, it was. Do you remember anything about them?"

"The faces kept changing, but there were three who seemed to be the main people. Two guys and a girl. The main man was called Drone and the girl was called Dusty. I hadn't thought of them in years. Jason and I went there a lot. I never took Tim."

"How come I never knew about this?" I asked.

"You were a goody two-shoes and didn't smoke pot," she replied.

The food arrived and Judy pounced on it like she was starving. I picked at mine and ate slowly, just to be bitchy. Just as we finished eating my cell phone rang.

"Hello," I answered into the phone. I listened quietly and then hung up.

"That was Tim Mallory," I said and watched as her face lit up. "The medical examiner just called. The remains in my backyard belong to Helga Johanson. The dental records proved it."

It might have been my imagination, but I could swear that she looked panicked, rather than shocked and sad.

I called Tim on my cell phone as I was heading back from Portland. He agreed to meet me after he got off work. It was summer time and the traffic was heavy with tourists. It took me longer to get home than I expected. Argus was grateful to get out of his crate and go for a short walk. I was making dinner when Tim drove up.

"Just in time for dinner," I said as he stepped into the house.

"Timing is my strong point," he replied.

"I've noticed," I said smiling. I was cooking up ham steak with mashed potatoes and turnip greens. As always, Argus was under my feet.

"Smells good," Tim said as he looked over my shoulder.

"Sit down at the table and take a look at the yearbook. Take a careful look at the candid photos of us at The Bridge. See if you see what I see."

"I don't see anything special," said Tim.

"Look at Bitch Blair. What is she wearing?" I asked.

"Shit, I didn't see that at first. How did you notice that?" he asked.

"Only because I'm the one who found it." We both looked at the photo again. There was no doubt. Judy Blair was wearing a peace medallion that was very familiar and distinctive. It looked exactly like the one I had uncovered in the back yard.

"There could have been hundreds of them at the time," said Tim, though he didn't sound convinced.

"Maybe," I said, "maybe not. I think Bitch Blair knows something about this." I told him about my trip to Portland and my lunch with Judy. He wrote down the information I gave him about the hippies named Drone and Dusty.

"I'll check into this and see what I can find out," Tim promised.

"By the way," I added. "Judy said she wouldn't mind renewing your acquaintance, if you know what I mean."

"Tell her I have a war injury."

"Which war?" I asked.

"War of the sexes. Her side lost!"

Dinner was ready and we ate in near silence as Argus slept on the floor under the table. We were both thinking about Helga. It was beginning to hit me that the skull I found was someone I had known and liked. I remembered my *Hamlet*. Prince Hamlet had picked up a skull in the graveyard and then been told it was the skull of Yorick, someone he had known as a child. It was an eerie and unsettling feeling.

I took the yearbook and went into the second bedroom I was using as an office and made a copy of the photo and sent a fax while Tim made the coffee. We went out to the porch with coffee and a slice of the honey molasses cake I had made.

"Are you okay?" asked Tim.

"I guess, just difficult to process something this evil." We sat on the porch and watched the night settle in.

At six in the morning, I was in the kitchen scrambling eggs when the phone rang. Tim picked it up.

"It's for you," he said as he handed me the phone.

"Oh, my God!" exclaimed Rhonda. "Who was that? Is that the cop? Have you been holding out on me? What's going on?" I held the receiver away from my ear until she was done.

"I'll tell you later, I'm sure you didn't call me at six am to check up on my breakfast companions. What's up?" I asked.

"Have you seen the *Portland Press Herald* this morning?"

"Not yet."

"The headlines read: 'Body Identified: Decades Old Murder' and then the story goes on about how you found the remains and now it turns out that it's someone you know. And there's a picture of her and you and a group of other kids. And not only that, but you remember that medallion you found? Well, one of the other kids is wearing it."

"I know, it was me who faxed the picture to the *Press Herald*," I stated.

"You did? Why?"

"I'll explain it all when I get to work."

"Fine, but this better be good," she said and hung up.

"Sorry about that," I said to Tim as I handed the phone back to him.

"Why did you fax the picture to the newspaper?" he asked.

"Well, Judy Blair is wearing the medallion. The medallion was in my back yard near the body. Judy lives in Portland. I wanted Judy to see the picture of her. If she is involved in any way, this is going to make her very nervous."

"Wow!" said Tim. "You are a devious bastard!"

. . . .

Argus and I walked into Erebus at about nine o'clock. Brad Watkins was at the counter and Rhonda was in the back room. I filled her in about all that had happened in the last few days.

"You are a fast worker, in all aspects," she said when I had finished.

"So what's up with you and Jackson Bennett?" I asked.

"Well," she began, "we've gone out twice and I think this might be going somewhere."

"Good for you. How's your sister?" Did I dare ask?

"She's going back to New York tomorrow, thank God! I can't stand another minute with her."

"Bring her over tonight for dinner. That way you won't be left alone with her."

"That's a great idea, Jesse, thanks."

I went to the computer and checked email orders and correspondences. There wasn't that much to do, and I really wasn't in the mood to sit inside all day. Summer is too short in Maine to waste, so I try to be outside as much as possible. Argus was more than ready to leave, and we headed down Front Street.

"Hey Ashworth!" It was Jason Goulet in a red convertible getting ready to pull out of a parking spot. "Want a lift?"

"Why aren't you working?" I asked.

"Taking the day off and going to Popham. Want to come along?" Popham Beach is one of Maine's best-kept secrets, a white sand beach in an undeveloped area. It's very beautiful, but even in summer the survival time in the ice-cold Atlantic Ocean is about seven minutes.

"Sure, I just need to drop Argus off at the house. I don't think dogs are welcome on the beach until fall."

"Hop in and I'll drive you home. We can have lunch at Spinney's"

"Spinney's is still there?" I asked. Spinney's was a little restaurant at Popham that we used to go to back when we were in high school.

"It's still there, hasn't changed, unlike us."

At home I grabbed a towel, swim suit, and a beach blanket. Argus, seeing all the activity, ran into his crate and curled up for a nap. Jason and I headed south into Phippsburg and Georgetown toward Popham Beach. Spinney's was just opening as we got there. We both ordered burgers and fries. After lunch we climbed the unfinished tower of Fort Popham and enjoyed the sweeping view. Then we walked along the beach and found a place to spread our towels and soak up some sun.

"It was quite a shock finding out that Helga was the one you found, even though we all suspected it," began Jason. "I wonder if we will ever find out the truth about what happened. The paper implied a link to you, Jesse, since you found the remains and had known her."

"We all knew her. The question is who was the last person to see her? It was so long ago that I doubt we'll ever know the truth. Did you ever hang

94

out at Eagle's Nest? Apparently there were hippies living there. Two names that came up were Dusty and Drone. Do you remember them?" I asked.

"I hadn't thought about them in years. Judy and I used to go there to buy dope," said Jason.

"Do you remember anything about them?"

"Drone worked at the shipyard as a painter. Dusty used to work at Ma Roy's store. That's about all I know," replied Jason.

"Are there records you could check in the accounting department from that long ago?' I asked.

"Yes, but I have no idea where to start looking. Drone wouldn't be his real name. And I don't know exactly when he worked there. But I'll have a look around," he promised. Just then, a group of giggling teens walked by.

"Remember being that young?" I asked.

"No, I never thought about us being young. I think we always thought we were adults.

"I think you're right," I stated. "Did Helga hang out with the hippies a lot?"

"I believe so," answered Jason. "She always seemed to be there. I think she was the girlfriend of one of the other guys there. She said the hippies reminded her of the young people back in Denmark. I know she did drugs, but I don't know what types she used."

"What was around back then?" I asked. I really didn't know much about drugs until I went to college.

"Mostly grass. Maybe some LSD. Speed was around some. But pretty tame stuff compared to what's around now."

95

"Well, you can really get messed up on any of those things. Put in some alcohol," I said, "and you have a full-fledged party. Anything else you remember about Helga or the hippies?"

"Pretty much that's all. I haven't thought about any of this until you excavated your back yard," answered Jason.

I had learned about as much from Jason as I was going to. We decided to take a walk down the beach and then head back to Bath. The ocean waves made a gentle lapping sound against the sand. The sun was warm and the light had a brilliance that heightened all the colors. I could smell the salt in the air and hear the cry of the gulls above. We walked in companionable silence. It was good to be alive.

Jason dropped me off at the house; I rescued Argus from his crate and took him for a walk. Just as we were returning, state investigators Jack Bradley and Amanda Gower pulled up in a big black car.

"Good afternoon, Mr. Ashworth. We would like to ask you a few questions," said Ms. Gower as Bradley looked on.

"Sure, have a seat," I indicated the chair on the porch. I wasn't about to invite them in for tea.

"Thank you," replied Bradley. "When was the last time you saw Helga Johanson?" He was frowning.

"The last time I remember seeing her was at our high school graduation, which was June tenth of that year."

"Do you remember anything significant about her around that time?" asked Gower. She smiled at me encouragingly. Was this their version of good cop/bad cop?

"No more than I've already told you."

"Where were you after graduation, when she disappeared?" Bradley was still frowning when he spoke.

"I left the morning after graduation with a friend. We went to Montreal for a week."

"Can anyone verify that?" asked Gower still smiling.

"The friend I was with is chief of police Mallory. I'm sure he'll tell you," I said, rather hotly. Bradley closed his notebook abruptly and shot out of the chair like he had been slapped.

"We'll be in touch," he growled.

"Good night Mr. Ashworth," cooed Gower.

Chapter 12

Rhonda and her sister Janice were due for dinner soon, and I didn't have anything ready. The visit from Gower and Bradley had upset my schedule, so I decided to serve some typical pub grub. I threw a salad together and I made shepherd's pie. The recipe was easy enough. I had copied it from an Irish pub in Boston where I used to go; they had taken the traditional recipe and tweaked it. I tweaked it even more and liked the result. I'd serve it with Seadog Summer Ale.

Tim called to see how I was after my visit with the investigative team. He also gave me a bit of information not released to the public yet. Helga Johanson had most likely died from a blow to the head. He asked me not to tell anyone until it was released to the public. I didn't think that would be an issue. Violent death was not great dinner conversation. Because he was working the next several nights I wouldn't see him until the weekend.

Rhonda and Janice showed up at my door just as I was putting dinner in the oven. I poured them both a beer and we went out to sit on the screen porch while dinner was cooking. I filled them in on my visit from Gower and Bradley. "I think they wanted to pin it on me to wrap this all up in a neat bundle. Fortunately I have a good alibi. I think they were little disappointed."

"Well," said Janice, "I can see what they were thinking. You buried the body and you found the body. It would make their life easier. Now they have to do some real work and investigate."

"And," added Rhonda, "they may never be able to solve this. Whoever did this, and we don't even know what they did, may be dead themselves after thirty-five years."

"I need to know for my own peace of mind," I said. "It was my back yard she was in, and she was my friend. For all I know she may have been killed by someone I know."

Rhonda was about to say something when my phone rang. I hate phones. They ring at the most inopportune time and they are very insistent. I left to answer the phone. After a brief conversation I went back out to the porch.

"Sorry about that," I apologized. "That was Becky Simpson inviting me to dinner tomorrow night." I turned to Janice to explain. "Bill and Becky Simpson were high school lovers from my graduating class. You met them here the other night."

"Oh yes," frowned Janice. "They were two of the most boring people on the planet I've ever met."

"And," added Rhonda, "I think she is wound just a little too tight."

"My thoughts exactly," I put in. "I want to get Bill alone and find out what he knows about Helga. Becky was just a little too nasty about her." I went to check on dinner. I looked in the oven and the gravy from the meaty bottom layer had bubbled up through the potato layer, a sure indication that it was done. I took it out of the oven to cool while I threw the salad together.

"Dinner is ready," I called out. I poured more beer and we sat down to eat.

"Jesse is the king of comfort food," Ronda told Janice.

"I prefer to call myself a white trash cook," I informed them.

"Honey, you call yourself anything you want, but this is divine!" stated Janice. "You come up with more recipes, and I'll find you a publisher."

"Done!" I said. "But I don't have any gourmet recipes. All those in my recipe box are simple dishes with only a few ingredients."

"There are too many fancy cookbooks. People want simple recipes they can actually make. When I get back to the office, I'll send you publishing guidelines."

"Can't wait," I said. We'll see if she ever does. I wasn't going to hang around waiting.

"I'm recruiting for the All Soul's softball team, and I need you on it," Rhonda turned and addressed me. "We're playing Holy Trinity on July fourth and having a picnic. I'm putting you down for left field and macaroni salad."

"I haven't played softball in years," I answered back. "Do I have a say in the matter?"

"No," said Rhonda, "you don't! It's only for a few hours and you need to get out and do stuff." I've learned over the last few decades that it's easier to go along with Rhonda than not. And I actually like to play softball, so my reluctance was more to annoy her than anything else. The rest of the evening was pleasant, and we stayed up late talking.

Chapter 13

In August of 2001 I arrived in Manhattan sometime around midnight on a train bound for Washington, DC. I remember looking out of my compartment and seeing the New York skyline ablaze in lights just before we entered the train station. Sometime later we pulled out of the city, and I saw the World Trade Center Towers standing tall over lower Manhattan.

A month later my students and I watched in stunned silence as the twin towers collapsed in a heap of rubble. As I observed my students I realized that the world had changed forever. Later in the day I walked through the cafeteria, and I experienced something that was truly terrifying. The normally boisterous lunch period was silent. Nothing has frightened me more as a teacher than the silence of that day. We had lost something that day.

Now, years later, I was experiencing again some of that feeling of loss. My memories of the carefree days of high school had been disturbed. A member of my class was murdered just days after graduation and buried only a few yards away.

I made myself busy in an effort to forget about Helga's death. After all, I really couldn't do anything about it or change what had already happened. I made a batch of sweet potato biscuits, harnessed up Argus and headed out to Erebus for the day. Rhonda was driving her sister to the airport in Portland and wouldn't be in until later. Brad Watkins and I would be in charge of the shop for most of the day.

Brad worked the shop while I worked at the computer. At break time we sat and had coffee and biscuits and we exchanged stories of Morse High then and now. Brad was a good student and would go far in life. Talking to him made me realize how hard it would be in September when school started without me.

Today was turning out to be a real bummer, and I wasn't looking forward to spending the evening with Bill and Becky Simpson. My biorhythms must be way off, that's the only thing I could blame.

"What's wrong?" asked Rhonda when she came into the shop at a little past noon.

"Why do you ask that?" I wondered aloud.

"Because I know you, and you've got that look."

"What look?" This was a game we played several times a year.

"What is it?" she asked again.

"I woke up thinking about nine-eleven. I think this whole Helga murder thing stirred up some deeper feelings of helplessness. There's not much I can do. I ask questions and the answers lead to more unanswered questions, and I don't think we are ever going to find out what happened to her."

"And if this was happening to me instead of you, what advice would you give me?" she asked.

"I'd tell you that answers come in unexpected ways in their own time," I answered.

"Now," said Rhonda, "Give me some of those biscuits over there and no one gets hurt."

. . . .

I stopped at the store on the way home and bought some wine. I hadn't had time to make anything to take to the Simpson's and it was either wine or flowers. The wine was easier to find and cheaper.

Argus and I took a nap before my evening out. I wasn't looking forward to the dinner at all, but it would give me a chance to ask some questions. I was hoping to get Bill alone without Becky. I had a few questions for him.

I took Argus for a walk, put him in his crate, grabbed the wine, and headed out the door. The evening was hot and humid, and I was expecting a thunderstorm. I arrived exactly at six o'clock and rang their doorbell. I waited and no one came to the door. I checked my watch. Whenever someone doesn't show up on time, I automatically think it's me who screwed up. I knocked on the door and I heard some scuffling from inside.

"Come in, Jesse," said Bill as he opened the door. "I should have told you that the doorbell doesn't work."

I handed him the wine. "I think we are in for a thunderstorm." As usual, when I can't think of anything to say, the weather is always an appropriate subject.

"Feels like it," responded Bill. "Hey, Becky, Jesse's here!"

"Hi, Jesse," greeted Becky as she came into the living room. She was wearing cut off jeans and a top that was clearly designed for a younger and thinner woman. I took a moment to look around the room. It was what is kindly called eclectic style in decorating magazines. The decorations were from the seventies. I was impressed that someone still had macramé wall hangings.

"Hi. Becky. Thanks for the invitation. It's always great to meet with old friends. Nice house," I lied. From where I stood I could see into the dining room and there was, honest to God, a paint-by-number painting of the Last Supper!

"Thanks. We've been collecting American folk art for years," Bill informed me.

"So I see." I had visions of yard sale after yard sale as these two collected their 'folk art.'

Bill took the wine into the kitchen and returned with filled glasses. We sat and exchanged pleasantries. Becky brought out what looked like crackers and cheese whiz as an appetizer. If I had enough wine, I told myself, these might even taste good.

"Well, said Bill, "I should go start up the grill."

"I'll go with you," I offered. It would give me a chance to talk to Bill alone.

"You boys go ahead. I'll bring out the food in a while," said Becky.

We went through the tiny kitchen into the backyard. Bill lifted the cover off the grill and ignited the gas, and we sat in the lawn chairs in the yard. The yard was small, but pleasant and well used. I wasn't sure how to begin my questions so I just dove right in.

"You heard that the remains were identified as Helga's?" I asked.

"You'd have to be dead yourself not to have heard it. It's all the papers have been reporting."

"I know," I said. "I really liked her. She was kind and very bright."

"And very pretty," added Bill. "I think she was the best looking girl at school. And she wasn't stuck up either. She even would smoke a joint now and then. And she liked the boys."

"Becky didn't seem to have anything nice to say about her when you two were at my house the other night," I said, hoping to keep him talking.

"That's because Helga and I had a thing going, and Becky found out about it. We used to go smoke dope with some hippie types and we crashed there a few nights. When Becky found out she was furious. She wouldn't talk to me for days."

This was getting interesting. "Did you know a guy named Drone who used to live in my house?" I asked.

"Drone and Dusty? Wow, that's a flash from the past. Yes, I used to hang out sometimes with Helga. I took Becky there a few times, too. It was Bath's version of Haight-Ashbury. It was free love, free food, and lots of dope. How do you know about Drone and Dusty? I didn't think you'd ever been there."

"Jason told me about them," I said.

"Jason?" Bill looked puzzled. "I don't remember seeing him there. "Of course, that was decades ago. I must say you certainly fixed up the house. It doesn't look anything like it used to look."

"Yes," said Becky as she stepped out into the backyard. "You've done wonders with that wreck of a place." I wondered how long she had been listening to us. She was carrying a platter of raw chicken that she passed to Bill. He took some tongs and placed the pieces on the grill.

When the chicken was done it was served with potato salad and green beans. We spent the evening talking about their jobs and all the good flea markets and yard sales that take place every summer. To be polite they did ask me some questions about my teaching career and travel, but for the most part they appeared to be completely boring and self-absorbed, not that I'm one to be judgmental you understand.

I was glad when it was sufficiently late that I could excuse myself. I'd have to write a thank you note tomorrow. I still write thank you notes, but it seems to be a dying art. My mother always made me write notes, and it was something I learned to do. That reminded me I hadn't heard from my parents in Florida in about a week. I'd better call them tomorrow and tell them about Helga.

Argus was glad to see me when I got home. He quickly ran out to the back yard, did his business, curled up in my lap and fell asleep. I sat in the chair reading and sipping Moxie until after midnight. I was beginning to like this retirement gig.

Chapter 14

The morning was very cool for the end of June. I was used to much warmer summer days, but it was pleasant to live once again without air conditioning. I have lived here now for about three weeks, and I realized I had yet to spend a complete day at the house. I was planning on spending the whole day here, but plans can change.

I made some coffee and thawed out some pancakes from the freezer. I like to cook, but I hate to cook in the morning, so I always make up large batches of pancakes and waffles and put them in the freezer. In fact I freeze a lot of food that I make ahead, because I never learned to cook for just one, so it was either freeze the leftovers or eat the same thing all week.

Tim called to check in and I told him that I had some more information about Helga, but nothing major. We planned to get together tomorrow and look at all the facts of the case. I spent the rest of the morning dusting and vacuuming, and then I finished by scrubbing the toilet. Housework was just a collection of delights!

The mail came a little after lunch and in it was a package from Rhonda's sister Janice. The package contained manuscript guidelines for cookbooks. Maybe she was serious. If nothing else I could collect and revise the recipes and have them printed locally. I knew Rhonda would sell them in her shop. It was a project I could have some fun with.

"What do you think, Argus?" I asked the dog. Argus looked at me and wagged his tail, but didn't answer. Sometimes he has to take time and think things through.

I got out some of the old recipe collections I bought at flea markets. I'd start with some old cookbooks that some local churches published years ago. These collections of old family recipes were invaluable. They were leftovers from a day when Maine women spent long hours in the kitchen trying to feed their families. In the days before supermarkets, they often had only a few ingredients to work with. I would have to test them and modify the recipes for today's more healthy lower fat diets. But it would be fun.

My recipe box was also valuable as a resource. I had collected and changed these over the years, plus they had the added benefit of having already been tested. My overall theme was going to be comfort food, but with a twist toward healthier ingredients. I would start each recipe with a comment on its history.

Working with the recipe cards gave me an idea. I always taught my students to take notes on index cards when they were writing a research paper. Then they could shuffle them around and put them in some sort of order. I began to write down all I had learned of Helga's murder on index cards. It would be helpful when Tim came over, because we could look for patterns or missing pieces. I'm easily distracted, so I worked on the index cards for about an hour before I got back to the recipes.

By three o'clock it was time for a Moxie break and some serious porch sitting. Argus curled up in my lap for a snooze as I sat enjoying the afternoon. I figured Argus had tired himself out from all the napping he did in the morning. Down the street I could see John Lowell mowing his lawn. He was using an old reel push mower; I hadn't seen one of them since I was a kid and even then most of us had gas mowers.

I hadn't bothered to put my car in the garage last night, so it was in the driveway. I noticed how dirty it was. I'd have to look around for a car wash, as I hadn't really bothered to look for one yet. Suddenly I saw something on my car. It was a piece of paper placed under my windshield wiper. I shot off the porch with Argus running behind me. I picked up the paper and unfolded it. In magic marker someone had printed "MYOB!" in big black letters. It took a few seconds for it to register that MYOB meant Mind Your Own Business!

Was I making someone nervous?

I looked around to see if I could see anyone in the vicinity, but the only person in sight was John Lowell. I put Argus on a leash and headed up the street.

"Good afternoon, John, looks like you've got quite a large job there." I said by way of greeting.

"Oh, hello Jesse," he returned. "I like to mow my own lawn; I've been doing it since the fifties."

"It's not my favorite chore. I keep waiting for someone to develop a strain of grass that's thick, but only grows to three inches. By the way, have you seen anyone near my car today?" I asked.

"Nope, not a soul. The only person I've seen all day was someone going by on a bicycle. But I didn't have my glasses on so it could have been anyone. Why do you ask?"

"No reason really," I answered. "I just thought I saw someone out there." No need to tell him about the note.

"Jesse, is that you?" yelled Mrs. Lowell from her front door. "John, bring Jesse in here. I've got some coffee made and some molasses cookies." I hesitated, but only for a moment. If I had the cookies, I could just walk a few miles to burn off the calories. I wasn't sure about having coffee after a can of Moxie, but I figured my kidneys were in pretty good shape, so what the heck.

By the time I arrived home I had forgotten about the note and spent the rest of the day poring over old recipes. By evening I had quite a collection of material for a cookbook. The problem wouldn't be finding recipes, but winnowing out the best ones and trying to come up with a focus. I wasn't sure anyone else would be interested in a cookbook of comfort food, but I would give it my best.

Chapter 15

My family did not come over on the Mayflower. In fact they were considered latecomers because they did not arrive on these shores until 1632 by way of Boston. I'm told they were fairly well off when they came here, but their fortunes must have diminished in the centuries that followed because I certainly never saw any family wealth. I did, however, inherit their good health and, I hope, their longevity. Unfortunately I inherited their tendency toward an increasing waistline, and so I started the day with an early morning jog to keep my waist at thirty-four inches.

It was going to be a hot day, I could tell, even though it was only six am. I wasn't sure this was going to be a good day to cook, so I planned to suggest to Tim that we meet for lunch at some air-conditioned restaurant. Afterwards we could go back to my place and take a look at the information we collected about Helga. I showered, made some dry toast and coffee, and worked in the garden until it became too hot to work. By lunchtime it was close to ninety degrees outside and there was no breeze in the air.

When I got into my car I remembered about the note I found under the wiper blade. Mind my own business? Where's the fun in that? I spotted Tim's truck when I pulled into Zelda's restaurant. Zelda's restaurant was just outside of town. The décor was 1920's and tried to look like a speakeasy from that era. Tim waved at me from a corner table.

"Hey," he said.

"Hey, yourself. What's up?"

"Just waiting for my date to show up," he replied.

"Well," I said, "When he or she shows up, I'll make myself scarce." Then I filled him in on everything that I'd found out in the last few days. I gave him my idea about putting everything on index cards.

"That's a great idea," he said. "I've seen it done in old detective movies."

"I got the idea when I was shuffling recipe cards." Then I told him about the package from Rhonda's sister and my checking into recipes.

"Hey, I'll be your guinea pig. Anytime you need a taste tester, let me know," he offered. Then I told him about the note on my car.

"It's probably a prank," he suggested. "But, be careful, you may be making someone upset."

"You know," I said to change the subject, "I've never been to your house. In fact I don't know where you live." He gave me the address and I recognized it as one of several 1930's housing developments created for the shipyard workers. Most of them had been sold off as private homes now, but they still seemed small and close together, and rather boxy.

"It's all I could afford when I was starting out. It was only me and sometimes Jessica, when she wasn't with her mother. And I haven't had much time to fix it up." He sounded apologetic.

"Raising a daughter and working hard is what's important. I've never been one to be impressed by where people live," I replied.

"Well, I live a pretty unimpressive life," and Tim looked away when he said this. I wasn't sure where this was leading. The waitress came by and we ordered lunch. When we finished Tim grabbed the check and I didn't protest. We have a saying in Maine, don't offer if you don't mean it.

"Let's go back to my place and look at all the facts we have so far."

"Sure, and I'll get to see Argus, too." Argus adored Tim, but then Argus loved everyone.

Back at my place we opened two very cold beers and placed my note cards on the kitchen table. Tim looked at them for a few minutes and then switched them around.

"I don't see much here to help us," said Tim.

"Well, let's look at each card first, and then maybe something will jump out at us. I just feel that there is something here that we are not seeing."

The first card simply stated the fact that I found her remains back in May when I was digging a garden. Other facts on the card were the remnants of polyester polka dot material found at the site, and a peace medallion found nearby with the date 1969 scratched on it.

The next two cards concerned the dental records. The CD data disk of Dr. Jacobs identified her remains. A Rita Toliver, who had signed in at the records storage warehouse, may have stolen the original dental files. Rita Toliver signed in as an employee of Dr. Jacobs's son's office. According to Ben Jacobs no Rita Toliver worked for him.

"We need to find out who this Rita Toliver is," Tim said as he pointed to the card.

"Or," I suggested, "it might not be related to the case at all. Maybe she was looking for one of

Ben Jacobs's files. She may have had nothing to do with this at all."

Tim looked at me for a moment, and then quickly took all the cards and laid them out on the table. "I know what's missing! I just now realized it. We have one more person to question. Come on, we are going for a visit!"

"Visit who?" I asked.

"We are going to call on our high school English teacher. We are going to see old lady LaFond!"

We headed to Tim's pickup truck and when we had strapped ourselves in I asked, "Why are we going to see old lady LaFond?"

"She was the head of the student exchange program. She might have information that we don't know about. That is," Tim continued. "if she remembers anything."

"She is very, very old," I agreed. "Is she at the Old Folks Home?"

"You really are out of touch. The Old Folks Home changed its name years ago. It wasn't politically correct, I guess." The Old Folks Home was a beautiful old mansion in Bath's south end that was set high on a hill. I always thought it looked like a southern plantation. We all used to joke about going there when we got old. We always thought about it as a way Bath took care of its own when people got old and sick. They even had a huge monument in the cemetery that said "Old Folks Home" on it.

"I guess things have changed. Ma Roy's Store is gone, and the old opera house is gone. Wilson'

Drug Store is gone. Sometimes I think progress is overrated," I sighed.

"Sometimes, Jesse, I think you're right"

"So where are we going?"

"Old lady LaFond is at the Sagadahoc Nursing Home." In a few minutes we pulled into the parking lot of a modern institutional looking building. A receptionist directed us down the hall. The door was open and Mrs. LaFond was sitting in a rocking chair by the window. She looked very old and frail, and I was sure she didn't even know where she was. Tim knocked loudly on the door.

"Come in I'm not deaf!"

"Hello, Mrs. LaFond I'm Tim…"

"I know who you are Timothy Mallory. I'm old, not stupid. I can still read a newspaper."

"Hello, Mrs. LaFond," I said.

"Jesse Ashworth, I should say you've been in the papers too."

"Mrs. LaFond," Tim began, "Can you tell us anything about Helga Johanson that you remember? I know you were the head of the foreign exchange program at Morse High."

"Lovely girl, such a pity she was killed. She stayed with her American family, as we used to call it. Cliff and Anita Turcotte took in several exchange students while their two girls were in high school. They were a couple of years behind you two, I think. Anyway both the Turcottes are dead, and I've no idea where the two girls are."

"Who took her to the bus on the day she was supposed to leave?" asked Tim.

"That was me. She said goodbye to the family, and I picked her up and waited with her for the bus."

"Did she get on the bus?" I asked.

"I was there when the bus pulled in. It was a charter bus for the exchange program. It was picking up all the exchange students in Maine and taking them on a tour of the country. And yes, she did get on the bus."

"Do you remember the names of the Turcotte girls?" Tim took out his notepad.

"Of course! The oldest one was Donna and the younger one was Leigh. Both of them smart as whips. Almost as smart as you two dunces! I always thought you too should get together!"

"Why do you say that?" I asked her puzzled.

"I said I'm old, not stupid. I watch *Will and Grace* reruns."

I had nothing to add to that. What was there to say? Tim had turned an unusual shade of red.

"So Jesse, what are you doing for work?" Mrs. LaFond asked me.

"I just retired from teaching high school English."

"Good for you! Retire early before you begin to hate it."

"Did you ever hate it?" I asked.

"Not for one minute. I loved it all those years. But the world has changed. I could never do it now."

"That's why I left early. It's not even the kids. It's the parents. They'll even lie for their kids," I said.

"Yes, exactly what I've heard from everyone."

Tim cleared his throat. "Thanks for your time Mrs. LaFond"

"Come back and visit an old lady anytime."

We headed out to Tim's truck and neither of us said a word until we were out of sight of the nursing home. "That wasn't bad for a nursing home," I said. "But just think, you work hard all your life and that's where you end up."

"Well at least she still has all her marbles," Tim said as he drove along the road. "We need to find the Turcotte girls and see what information they can give us."

"They may not be easy to find. But I can check on the Internet and see what comes up. The girls, by the way, are fifty or older by now."

"It sounds so old, Jesse, and we are even older than that. Though you certainly don't look it."

"Or you either!" We both started laughing. "And for that compliment, I just might have some freshly baked cupcakes ready when we get home."

"You are awesome. We should get back to your place and rescue poor Argus."

Argus was excited to see us and jumped all over Tim when we got back to the house. My answer machine was blinking with two messages. I hate answer machines, but it seems to be a necessary evil in modern life. The first message was a hang up, and the second message was from Jason. "Hi, this is Jason. I found an employee record for Drone. Believe it or not that is really his name. Also I've got an interesting fact about him to tell you when I see you at the softball game tomorrow." I erased the message and made some green tea to go with the cupcakes. I put everything on a tray and took it out to the screen porch where Argus was curled up in Tim's lap.

I sat the tray down. "I just had a message from Jason Goulet. He said he had some interesting information about Drone, the hippie who used to live here. He said he would be at the game tomorrow."

"I almost forgot about the All Soul's softball game. I said I'd pick up potato chips for the picnic. What are you bringing?"

"I said I'd make a macaroni salad with my own homemade mayonnaise. Which means I need to get started on it now."

"You need any help?" Tim asked.

"Not in the kitchen, but you could help out in one or two other rooms later!"

Tim smiled. "No problem."

Chapter 16

The fourth of July began with a brilliant red sunrise and a light breeze. My grandmother used to say, "Red sky at morning, sailor take warning," but there didn't seem to be a cloud in the sky. I was up early at five. When I was young I couldn't wait for the time when I could sleep as late as I wanted. The cruel trick of nature is that as you get older you lose the ability to sleep late in the day, but you make up for it by napping in the afternoon. Tim had gone out to get a dozen doughnuts and a change of clothes. I like to cook, but really have no desire to make breakfast, and I was happy to eat doughnuts, even if they aren't good for you.

The town was all decked out for the fourth. Flags were flying everywhere and a carnival had set up operation in the waterfront park. There would be fireworks over the river after dark, and no doubt plenty of firecrackers going off before and after.

The game was going to be held in the Huse School ballpark. We were playing the Lutherans of Holy Trinity and, I hoped I wouldn't be the one to lose the game!

While I was waiting for Tim to return with the doughnuts, I put together the macaroni salad. The homemade mayo always impressed everyone. The secret is that years ago I found a recipe that was almost as easy as opening up a jar of store-bought, plastic tasting goo. Most recipes in cookbooks are unbelievably complicated with many steps. Mine is easy, add the ingredients together and stir in a double boiler. That's it, and the taste is superior to anything in the store.

"Chocolate, plain, or honey-dipped?" asked Tim as he handed me the dozen doughnuts.

"Yes, to all three," I said and poured the coffee.

"I met Rhonda at the pastry shop. You should see the getup she's wearing!"

"Oh, no," I replied, "It doesn't have feathers on it does it?"

"Yes it does, how did you know?"

"She dresses in red, white, and blue feathers on each fourth! Wait till you see what she wears on Christmas Eve!"

Before long it was time to go to the game. I packed the salad in a cooler and put it in Tim's truck. We dropped off the chips Tim bought and the salad at the church and headed to the Huse School field.

Rhonda was at the field when we got there. She had brought along Jackson Bennett as her date. He took his place on the bleachers. There were a lot of church people there. Bill and Becky Simpson were there to lend their support for the team. John and Dorothy Lowell had volunteered to take Argus with them. He was sitting with them in the bleachers and wagging his tail. He loves to watch outdoors sports! It was hard to tell which church had the most supporters, but I figured they were about equal. We probably had a much younger team than Holy Trinity, but it was hard to tell. We had Red Roberts, an octogenarian, who could probably run circles around me. The Reverend Mary Bailey and The Reverend Mark Christiansen offered up a prayer of thanksgiving for good fun and fellowship, then they tossed a coin to see which team would go first. We

Stephen E. Stanley

lost and Holy Trinity members lined up to bat. I got
to play the infield and Rhonda was the pitcher.

Rhonda started the pitch with both hands on
the ball before pitching underhand to the batter. Her
feathers were blowing in the wind and causing a
distraction for the other team. I'm sure she had that
in mind when she dressed up. The batter hit a fly ball
to the infield. I looked up and caught the ball for the
first out. The next batter hit the ball and made an
overrun to first base. The third batter looked like he
had just celebrated his one hundredth birthday, and
Rhonda took pity on him and walked him to first.
Reverend Mark was up and he cracked a home run.
Obviously he had done this before. Rhonda got
competitive and threw caution to the wind and struck
out the next two batters, and it was our chance to be
up.

Deacon Jane Foley was the first at bat and got
to first base. Rhonda was next and hit a fly ball, but
the infield did not catch it. My turn came next and I
hit the ball, advanced to first and now the bases were
loaded. Reverend Mary was up at bat and hit a home
run. I figured maybe they learned how to do that at
Reverend school!

By the fifth inning the score was five to five.
There was a distant rumbling of thunder and some
dark clouds advancing toward us from the west.
Suddenly a loud crack of thunder and a lightning
bolt filled the air around us. We quickly agreed to
call it a tie and both teams headed back to All Souls
for lunch in the parish house. Rain started to pelt us
as we scrambled to the parking lot. By the time we
arrived at All Souls it was pouring rain and the
thunder and lightning was truly frightening.

121

Just as we entered the parish house to prepare lunch a flash of lightening hit nearby and the lights went out. Members of the church quickly found some candles, and lunch was served by candlelight.

Rhonda, Jackson, Tim and I loaded our plates with fried chicken, chips and my macaroni salad. We sat at a large table with some parishioners of Holy Trinity. Both clergy persons offered a prayer and we dug in. The thunder and lightning was still going on outside the window.

"I guess my grandmother was right when she said 'Red sky at morning, sailor take warning,'" I said as another thunder boomer hit.

"Was the sky red this morning?" asked Rhonda. "I Slept in!" she said and giggled as she looked at Jackson. Rhonda actually giggled like a schoolgirl!

"Yes, it was very red." I responded trying to keep a straight face. Then I turned to Tim. "How is it you got the fourth of July off?"

"I'm the boss," he said. "But I'm on call. My second-in-command should be able to handle anything that comes up. By the way, I didn't see Jason here. Didn't you say he was coming?"

"I forgot all about it, but yes, he said he was coming to the game. Something must have come up."

"Great game to watch!" said Jackson Bennett "I especially liked watching the pitcher."

"Oh, stop!" said Rhonda, obviously pleased. Yes, stop! I thought to myself.

Tim's cell phone went off. He had it set to vibrate, but we could all hear it. He looked at the screen and then walked out into the hall to answer it.

We all continued our conversation at the table, remarking that the storm was passing over and that we would probably have a sunny afternoon. The rain had slowed down and there were patches of sun. Tim returned to the table looking pale.

"I have to go into work to attend to an incident. Jesse, would you walk out with me?"

"Sure," I answered. What was all this about?

Just as we got out of hearing range of the tables, Tim turned to me and said, "I just got a call from the station. There's been a shooting on Payne Road. Jason Goulet has been shot!"

. . . .

Have you ever noticed that tragedies happen on the most ordinary of days? When I was a student in elementary school the principal came on the intercom to announce that President Kennedy had been shot in Dallas. Up until then it was just an ordinary day. On another ordinary day I was preparing to give my sophomore class and vocabulary quiz, when Joyce Brown, who was on her way to teach a class, stopped by my classroom to say the space shuttle, with teacher Christa McAuliffe on board, had just blown up. On an ordinary day in 2001 I was surfing the Internet for teaching ideas during my free period when I stumbled onto a news page that reported that a jet had crashed into the World Trade Center.

The thing about ordinary days is that they are so ordinary that you are completely unprepared for tragedy. Today had not been just ordinary, but pleasant and safe feeling. It was a festive holiday. We were a church group playing softball with another church group. What could possibly happen? We were having an inside picnic together because of a thunderstorm, but we were warm and dry and safe, so when Tim told me about Jason Goulet being shot it was like a slap in the face.

"I don't have any of the details yet, I'll call you when I learn something more," Tim explained and then he was gone. I tried to go back to the table and pretend nothing had happened. Why upset everyone on such a good day when I didn't even have the facts? But as soon as I sat down Rhonda asked me what was wrong; it must have shown in my face.

"Tim had to go investigate a shooting." I made it sound vague because I didn't want to talk about it until I had more information. I stayed through dessert, but then collected Argus from the Lowells and we walked home. It was still raining, but I didn't really care if I got wet or not.

It wasn't until after nine in the evening that Tim called with news about Jason. Jason was taken by ambulance to Maine Medical Center in Portland. He had several gunshot wounds, but he was going to be all right. Tim was staying in Portland to talk to Jason after he came out of surgery. We still didn't have any details about the shooting, but at least Jason was expected to survive; the other details could wait.

The rain stayed with us into the next day. Argus hates the rain and needed a push out the door to do his morning business. He lifted his leg and did a fake pee and then raced back onto the porch.

"Nice try, Argus. Now get out there and do your business." I pointed to the wet lawn. Argus lowered his tail and headed out into the rain, did his business and raced back onto the safety of the porch with his tail wagging.

I really didn't want to spend the day alone, so I made up a batch of honey molasses muffins, packed them up, picked up Argus and carried him to the car. I drove to Erebus, parked the car and entered the back entrance. Rhonda was there in her office waiting to open the store for business. Argus took his spot under my desk.

"Muffins!" she cried. "You are a saint! I was just thinking about getting something good to eat. So what was going on that Tim left so quickly and then you walked home in the rain? Did you two have a fight?"

"Hardly," I said. Then I told her about Jason.

"Oh, my God! That's awful! Are you okay?" She reached for a muffin.

"I'll be better when I get the whole story." We chatted for a while and then started the workday. I inventoried the store and placed orders for new products. Rhonda's Internet business was doing very well, though in-store sales were somewhat slower. The biggest increase in business was from the New Age articles and books that she carried. We had just run out of Ouija boards and tarot cards.

Tim finally called a little before noon. Jason was able to give Tim a few details about the shooting. Jason was getting into his car and someone on a bicycle rode by and the next thing he knew he was being shot at. He had few details about the person on the bike, but he had a general impression that it was a woman. I remembered that when I found the note on my windshield that the Lowells saw a bicycle on my street. Could there be a connection?

Chapter 17

It was time to spend a day at home. I had been so busy the last few days that I decided to spend an 'at home' day. Eagle's Nest could use a good cleaning, and despite my best effort, it did not yet feel like home. I needed to cut the grass, weed the garden, plant some more perennials, and work on my cookbook. Argus needed some attention too, so I vowed not to leave the house today. After dusting, vacuuming, and washing the floors, I decided that the day was too hot to work outside. The garden would just have to keep for a cooler day.

As I was preparing to work on recipes at the kitchen table, I found the note cards that Tim and I were working on and looked through them. I had more information now and wrote up two more cards to add to the stack. Tim and I would go over them later.

We still had to find a lead to Donna and Leigh Turcotte. They must have known Helga better than anyone, seeing that she lived with them for the time she was here. I tried an Internet search, but it didn't pull up anything. Maybe Tim would have better luck using his police database.

While I was at the computer I pulled up some Maine news sites to read about Jason's shooting. They really didn't have any more information than I did, but I did read about the community's reaction to the shooting. Bath has very little crime and shootings happen very infrequently. There was an almost panicked response from some of the neighbors, fearing that this might be a random shooting. There were editorial calls for the police to be more proactive. Poor Tim must be taking the brunt of some of this.

I started working on my cookbook. I wrote an introduction to American chop suey. It came as a surprise to me that there are places in the United States that had never heard of this dish. It was created during the war to make use of easily obtained ingredients and to be easy to make after a hard day at the munitions factory. I have made this dish so often I had never even written down the recipe, so I had to stop and think about how to write it out. Argus was sleeping under the table while I worked on the cookbook. He looked up at me and barked and danced around. As I looked at the clock I realized that it was his supper time. Pugs have a surprisingly accurate internal clock.

"Hey, Argus, you want your supper?" I asked. That sent Argus into a fit of squealing and dancing until I got his dish ready, then he wolfed down his food.

Just as Argus was finishing his meal the phone rang.

"S'up?" I said in greeting.

"Hi, it's me." I recognized Tim's voice. "Jason is going to stay at Maine Medical Center for one more day. Then he should be ready to go home."

"Great, I'll plan to visit him tomorrow. You want to drive up with me?"

"Sure, I have to work in the evening, but I'll be free until four. I'll take you to lunch."

"Super, I'll pick you up around nine."

After Tim rang off, I really didn't feel like working, so I harnessed Argus up and we went for a walk. It was hot in the sun, but very comfortable in the shade. The air was very dry so that the heat wasn't oppressive. People in the neighborhood had done a great job with their gardens. July really was a great time of year. This was the first summer I can remember that didn't seem to be rushing by too quickly. I think the fact that, for me, not having to go back to school after Labor Day had a great deal to do with it.

Argus was beginning to pant, so we headed back home. Pugs do not like the heat and are susceptible to heat stroke, so it's always best to curtail their outside activities on warm days.

The view down the hill from Eagle's Nest was amazingly clear. I sat on the front porch with Argus sleeping at my feet. From here I could see the town and the river. I was getting hungry and wasn't sure what to get until I remembered the recipe I had just copied down. Then I remembered the section on American chop suey that I finished earlier! Life doesn't get any better than this, I thought to myself.

. . . .

The next morning I was able to find Tim's small detached brick house without any problem. As a kid I had lived in one just like it for several years. The difference was that ours had been attached to a row of townhouses, but it had been just down the street from where we were now. I remembered the coal furnace and wood cook stove that both sat in the small kitchen. Tim's house had been updated and had a modern kitchen. As he showed me around there was very little resemblance to the houses I remembered as a kid.

"This is nice, Tim," I said.

"Thanks, it was mostly fixed up when I bought it twelve years ago. I updated the kitchen appliances, but everything else had been done for me. It's fine for just me and Jessica, though it's so small, I can't really collect a lot of stuff."

He showed me his daughter's room. "It's disturbingly girlie, isn't it?" he asked. I had to agree as I looked at the pink walls and ruffled bed spread.

"When is she coming back?" I asked.

"End of the month, or whenever she has had enough of her mother."

We got in the car and I drove to Portland. The traffic on 295 was heavy and we were slowed down by the ever-present summertime construction.

"Doesn't anybody work?" I asked Tim as we looked at the congested traffic.

"If they do, I don't know when. There are always people on the roads, in the stores, and in the way."

Maine Medical Center has grown over the years and pretty much dominates the city skyline. We pulled into town and headed up Congress Street to the parking garage.

"Lead the way," I told Tim, as he had interviewed Jason and knew where his room was. We took the elevator to the street level, entered the hospital, and walked through long corridors and more elevators until we got to Jason's room. There was the ever-present hospital smell.

Jason was sitting up in bed and looked very frail and old. Jason smiled when he saw us and began to look better. "Mallory and Ashworth! What's up?" he greeted us.

"What the hell are you doing, Goulet, getting shot and spoiling our holiday?" I asked.

"Damn inconsiderate!" Tim muttered.

"Well, at least it got your attention," Jason smiled up at us. We sat down in the visitor chairs. Jason is not one to complain, so when he told us about the pain and the hospital food, we had to believe him. He gave us the details of the day he was shot. He was getting ready to go to our softball game and was heading to the car. He heard a pop and felt a pain in his shoulder. He twisted around and saw someone on a bicycle. The next thing he remembers was waking up in an ambulance. Tim had already asked him the questions about enemies, debts, and so on. No one seemed to have a motive.

"So what did you learn about our friend Drone. And could that have anything to do with you getting shot?" I asked.

"Just what I told you in the message I left on your answer machine on the morning of the softball game." Tim looked at me with a questioning look.

"I didn't get any phone messages from you," I said.

"Well, I left you a message and it was your voice on the machine. Very recognizable, too," Jason replied.

I was puzzled. "It must have malfunctioned," was all I could say about it.

"So what was the message?" Tim asked. This was all news to him.

"I checked the shipyard's personnel records and found out that Drone was a real last name and that his first name was Richard. I looked at the dates of his employment and knew that there were still some guys working who might remember him. That was when it became interesting. Steve Hartman was one of the guys who worked with Drone. He's Drone's cousin and he got Drone the job. Then it became really interesting. He told me that Drone is Judy Blair's older half brother. Her mother had been married before. Richard Drone is the child from her first marriage. Judy Blair is from the second marriage.

"Bingo!" I said.

"Holy shit!" said Tim.

"I never knew Judy had an older brother, and I never would have guessed that it was Drone. The times Judy and I went there, she was never treated any differently than anyone else," Jason informed us.

"Well," I said, "This adds another index card to our stack of information."

"The more information we get, the more confused this is all becoming. And does any of this really have anything to do with Helga Johanson's murder?" Tim asked.

We visited a while longer before we headed out for lunch. I agreed to come back tomorrow and pick up Jason and take him back to Bath. I offered to let him stay at my house until he recovered. Jason nodded in agreement and looked relieved. I drove down Congress Street and headed to the Old Port section of Portland.

"How's this for luck?" I asked Tim as I pulled the car into the only empty parking space on the street.

"I guess we were meant to be here," answered Tim. "What type of food do you want? Italian, seafood, or wicked fancy?"

"Wicked fancy? That sounds interesting. Let's do that!"

We walked down the brick sidewalk until we came to an old warehouse that had been updated into a very popular restaurant. The dining room was all done in stainless steel and glass furniture with exposed brick walls. We both ordered martinis and checked out the menu.

"Do you think that Jason being shot has anything to do with the Helga investigation?" I asked.

"Yes, I do. But I have no proof, just a gut feeling. We don't have many shootings in Bath. Maybe one or two shootings every other decade or so."

"None of this makes any sense to me." I sighed.

"We need to find this Drone dude and the Turcotte girls and see if we can get any answers."

The waiter returned and I ordered the crab cakes with seafood sauce. Tim ordered the sole fillet. We both ordered another martini.

"What happens to Helga's remains?" I asked Tim. "She has no family to claim them."

"I guess they just sit in a storage box somewhere." Tim frowned. I'd make a phone call tomorrow and find out.

We changed the subject and I talked about my years of teaching, and he talked about his years in the service and then his career as a cop. We had a pleasant ride back to Bath.

"I'm taking the night off!" Tim announced as I pulled into his driveway. "Why don't you go pick up Argus and come back for dinner? I'll cook."

"It's a deal," I answered. The only thing I like better than cooking for someone is when someone cooks for me.

Argus had been cooped up most of the day in his crate, so after I fed him I grabbed a bottle of dry white wine, and we walked the half-mile or so to Tim's house.

Tim was firing up the gas grill as we arrived and had picked out two good-sized steaks. I put the salad together while he grilled. Argus sat and watched Tim grill, hoping, I'm sure, that Tim would drop something on the ground.

We had a pleasant evening and never mentioned the Helga investigation at all. Argus found a comfortable place to nap, and Tim and I talked well past midnight. I was afraid we might run out of things to talk about. We never did.

The next morning I was hastily dressed and rummaging around in Tim's kitchen making a pot of coffee while Tim was in the bathroom. The door suddenly flew open and Jessica Mallory entered carrying two suitcases.

"Hey, Dad I'm..." she stopped suddenly and put down the suitcases as she saw me. "Mr. Ashworth?"

"Hi, Jessica I ..." I was flustered and didn't know what to say.

From the bedroom I heard Tim yell, "Hey, Ashes. I'm going to shower! Want to come and watch?"

"Ah, Tim? Your daughter is here."

Jessica was looking confused until Tim entered the kitchen wrapped in a towel. Confusion turned to shock.

"Well," I said to both of them as I snapped the leash on Argus. "I'm sure you both have a lot to talk about." I grabbed Argus and headed for the door. "Call me later," I yelled back as I headed out the door.

"I thought that went well!" I said to Argus as we headed up the street toward home. Argus just wagged his tail and kept on walking. Nothing but a missed meal could upset a pug!

Chapter 18

The morning news was full of stories about the hurricane that was expected to hit the coast of Florida sometime soon. Weather is something that we in Maine always listen to, even when it is far away. My parents and grandparents remembered the terrible storms that hit the New England coast in the 1930's, so most of us grew up paying attention to the weather. In my lifetime there were no hurricanes of the magnitude that so frightened the older generations, but I knew that hurricanes in the south usually came our way sooner or later in the form of rain.

I made coffee while I listened to the radio. I had left Tim's house before my morning coffee and I wasn't about to face the day without it. After a shower and some dry toast I got in the car to pick up Jason.

When I got to the hospital Jason was dressed and waiting to be discharged.

"I really appreciate your picking me up, Jesse."

"No problem. Have your heard from your kids?" I asked.

"Alan's called me every day I think. Julie has called a couple of times. Neither one seems inclined to hop on a plane and fly out here."

"I'm sure they're really busy," I said, not really believing it. "Besides, I'll bet you said it was really nothing."

I could tell by the look on his face that I had guessed the truth. Just then the nurse came in with a wheelchair ready to discharge him, and I went to pick up the car. He was still on powerful painkillers so he slept for most of the ride back to Bath.

When we got back to my place, I set Jason up in the guest bedroom and went to make us some lunch. Argus had curled up with Jason to keep him company. I checked my answer machine and there were two messages. I hate to see that message light flashing. I pushed the button. The first message was from Tim. "Hey, give me a call when you get in with Jason. I'll be at work." The second message was a hang up. That reminded me that I should check the machine, because I never got Jason's message. I checked the settings and they all seemed untouched.

I made egg salad sandwiches, opened a bag of chips, and set them on a tray with two cans of Moxie and took lunch in to Jason. He sat up in bed and I sat in the chair and we had lunch.

"Sorry, I'm not better company," said Jason.

"You'll feel better tomorrow. Those pain killers and pretty strong so take a nap and relax. You can stay here as long as you need to."

"Thanks, buddy."

"No problem. I have to go and call Tim now, and tell him we are safe and sound."

I left Jason to nap and went to call Tim. I cleaned out the dishwasher and put away the dishes until I realized that I was stalling so I wouldn't have to call Tim. I called the police station and was transferred to his office.

"Nice exit this morning, asshole" was Tim's greeting to me.

"We're fine, thank you for asking." I said in response.

"How's Jason doing?"

"He's still doped up from the pain killers, but I think he'll be fine in a day or two. And how are you doing?" I asked carefully.

"Jessica and I had a long talk this morning. She's glad I found someone to hang out with."

"Interesting word choice," I laughed.

"You know kids. They can't believe adults know about sex."

"Tell me about it. I taught high school kids, remember?"

Tim said he would be by later to see Jason and hung up. Argus came out of Jason's room looking for me, so I fed him and took him out for a walk.

We walked north on High Street toward town and passed Morse High. Since it was summer it had that forlorn look that most schools have when there are no students. The old 1929 building was almost swallowed up by the numerous new additions that had been added over the years. My class was one of the first classes to occupy the north addition that had almost doubled the space of the school. Since that time another major addition had been added; one that I had never been in. Argus loved all the smells in the front of the school and was quite happy to nose around the area.

From High Street we walked down Walker Street into the downtown area until we got to Erebus.

"Hey, Mr. Ashworth," greeted Brad Watkins when we walked into the shop.

"Hi Brad, I thought I'd get caught up on my work. Where's Rhonda?"

138

"She's having lunch with Mr. Bennett" Brad informed me.

"Good for her. Hey Brad, I just walked by Morse High. What's in the south wing of the school? I haven't been in there since I graduated."

"Classrooms, offices, and the cafeteria," he informed me. We never had a cafeteria when I was in school. We used to walk over to the Huse School and have lunch with the little kids. I remember having a meal called 'bubble and squeak' at least once a month. I had no idea what it was. I'd have to do some research and see if I could find the recipe.

"Are you looking forward to your senior year?" I asked him.

"Yes, but it's a little scary, too."

"The important thing is to just enjoy your last year. Work hard and have fun." The teacher in me couldn't shut up.

I went to the back room with Argus trailing behind me. I checked for online orders and then filled the few I had. I noted low inventory and placed orders for replacements, and then I filled some orders for shipments.

"How's Jason?" Rhonda had returned from lunch and poked her head in the back room. I filled her in on Jason and then gave her a report on orders and supplies.

"How was lunch?" I asked.

"Great! He took me to Zelda's. He's such a gentleman."

"I hope he's not too much of one, if you know what I mean," I said.

"Don't you worry about me, sweetie."

"I'm more worried for Jackson. Poor bastard doesn't know what he's dealing with." I teased.

"You got that right!" said Rhonda. "Now, in case you have forgotten this is pension pay day. You should be getting your first check in the mail." I had forgotten about it. "And, just to make it interesting I have a paycheck for your work here at Erebus too!"

"Oh God, I'm rich!" I said as she handed me the check. "Now that you've paid me I think I'll go home and check on Jason."

On the walk back to Eagle's Nest with Argus, I watched the clouds come slowly in and block out the sun. By the time we got to the house it was dark and stormy looking. I looked in on Jason. He was asleep and so I took a book and sat down in an easy chair for a quiet evening. It turned out to be not as quiet as I would have liked.

I must have dozed off because suddenly there was a loud clap of thunder, and I was out of the chair and standing in the middle of the room. Argus jumped up with me and started barking. I checked in on Jason, and he was awake, but not too lively. I went into the kitchen and fixed up two plates of leftovers for supper.

I brought the plates into the guest room and sat in a chair while Jason ate on a tray. I told him about my day, just to keep conversation going. He still seemed foggy, and apologized. I said not to worry and just rest up. I grabbed the dirty dishes and headed to the dishwasher. The phone rang as I entered the kitchen. When I answered it there was no one there. I checked the caller ID but it said "Unavailable." I assumed it was a telemarketer on an automated system.

Outside it was becoming darker and the lightning flashes and thunder were getting closer. The lights were beginning to flicker and just as the lightning struck again the lights went out all together. I moved to the kitchen and found a flashlight and lit up a kerosene lamp. Maine houses always have one or two kerosene lamps around. Though they appear to be for decoration, they have a real and necessary function.

Once I got some lights on in the house I went to the front porch to see if I could see any lights from town. Everything was dark, which meant that it wasn't just my house that had no power, but the whole town. Just as I entered the house again the phone rang. I picked up the cordless phone and then realized that it wasn't going to work without power. The ringing was coming from the kitchen on the corded phone. I picked it up, said hello, and got no response. Just as I was about to hang up I heard a muffled voice say "Mind your own business!" and then they hung up. I couldn't tell if the voice was a man or woman because of the whispered and muffled message. I went to check the caller ID and then realized that if the cordless phone didn't work, neither would the caller ID on the phone.

Jason appeared in the doorway looking sleepy. "What's going on?" he asked.

"The thunder storm knocked out the power, that's all."

"That thunder sure was loud. It woke me up."

There was a knock on the door and Tim stepped into the room, still dressed in his uniform. "I saw lights and thought you might have power. It's out all over town. Hey Jason, I'm glad to see you up and around."

"I just got up," replied Jason.

"How are you doing?" Tim asked.

"The pain pills have knocked me on my ass, but the pain isn't really bad."

"I think," I added, "That I have some chocolate cake somewhere if anybody is hungry." We sat and had some cake and tea by lamplight in the kitchen. The great thing about a French cook stove is that you can boil water even during a power outage because it uses gas. We sat in silence after we each gave a report about our day. The thunder had moved up the coast, but we could still hear it rumbling in the distance.

"How long does the power usually stay off after a storm?" I asked just to make conversation.

"Anywhere from an hour to three days," said Jason. "Good to see you Tim, but I need to go back to sleep."

"See you in the morning," I said to Jason.

"Poor bastard," said Tim when Jason was out of sight. "It must hurt like hell."

I told Tim about the phone call. "You need to be careful," he said. "You don't know what you are getting into."

"It's probably a wrong number," I said lamely.

"Oh sure it is," Tim replied. "I should go in to work. With the lights being off the police station will be a madhouse. Every old lady in the city will be calling and every yuppie's alarm system will be going off."

"I never thought of that. Stop by tomorrow if you get a chance."

"I will. I'm off tomorrow." And with that he was gone. The house was very quiet. It always amazes me in a power outage how quiet the house can be. We are so used to the background noise of modern life that silence is a shock.

I checked in on Jason, who was fast asleep, then locked up the house, blew out the candles, and turned in for the night. Sometime in the middle of the night the lights came back on. I know because I think every light in the house had been switched on, plus the TV had reset itself and was running. I got up and turned the lights and the TV off.

I tossed and turned for a while, but I couldn't get back to sleep. Something was bothering me, but I couldn't put my finger on it. I had a feeling that something was really wrong, but I chalked it up to my imagination. I decided to go sit out on the screen porch in the back of the house. I figured the night air might make me sleepy. Argus came with me and we settled into a chair, and I put my feet up on the ottoman. I must have dozed off because Argus was restless and woke me up.

I could smell it before I saw it. There was a smoky smell in the air. I couldn't tell immediately where the flames were coming from. I stepped off of the porch to look around and then I saw it! There were flames coming from my garage! My garage was on fire!

Chapter 19

Nothing wakes up a neighborhood faster than a fire truck with sirens and flashing lights at four in the morning. By the time the firefighters had my garage fire under control, there was a crowd of about twenty-five people milling around in my driveway. Tim was out there doing crowd control. He had shown up shortly after the fire department.

The damage hadn't been much, but it was clear that someone had set the fire. I had luckily left my car parked in the driveway, so the only actual damage was to the north corner of the garage. Tim said someone had left a candle burning in a box filled with oily rags. When the candle burned down, the rags caught fire. This gave the fire starter an hour or so for getaway time. The damage was slight because it was caught in time. If I had been sleeping it would most likely have been a total loss.

By seven o'clock everyone had gone home except for Tim. I was serving coffee, scrambled eggs and ham with cornmeal muffins. Nothing like a little garage fire to stimulate the appetite. Jason came into the kitchen when he smelled the coffee. Apparently he had slept through the whole ordeal. The three of us sat down to breakfast and Tim and I filled Jason in on all the excitement he missed.

"How are you feeling today, by the way? " I asked.

"Much better today, I think. The pain is less and I'm going to try not to take the pain killers unless I need them."

"You're passing up drugs?" Tim asked. Jason had been known to do drugs back in high school.

"I don't do drugs anymore. When I became a father, I gave up drugs. It was for the kids."

"I know what you're saying," agreed Tim.

"When I'm healed up, the three of us should go out looking for some hot chicks," said Jason with a wink.

"Eat your breakfast," I snapped at him to change the subject.

"Ah, Jason," Tim began, "There's something we should tell you." Tim filled him in on why we wouldn't be joining him down at the singles bar.

"Holy shit!" said Jason. "That explains a lot." The he burst into a fit of laughter. "Holy shit!" he kept repeating until he was gasping for air.

"I'm glad we could be your morning entertainment," I said when he had stopped laughing. Jason got up and gave us both a hug before bursting into laughter again.

"I think I'll take those drugs after all," Jason said as he left the room.

"Well, that went well don't you think?" I asked Tim.

"Poor, sorry bastard," was all Tim could say.

About midmorning I called the insurance company and reported the fire in my garage. They weren't happy about the fact that someone set it. Tim wasn't happy either and warned me to watch myself. He would be by tomorrow on his day off and we would go over events and see if we could discern some type of pattern.

Jason was well enough today to sit up and watch some TV, so I left a lunch plate for him in the refrigerator, packed up the rest of the corn muffins,

put the harness on Argus and headed out to work at
Erebus.

"Good morning, Mr. Ashworth," greeted
Brad Watkins when I entered the shop.

"Brad, call me Jesse. You remind me of one
of my students when you call me Mr. Ashworth.
Here have a corn muffin," I said as I handed him the
bag. "Where's the old bitty?"

"I heard that!" yelled Rhonda from the back
room.

"What did you hear? The old bitty part or the
corn muffin part?"

"The corn muffin part. I am an old bitty, and
if I don't get my blood sugar up, I'm going to be a
cranky old bitty." Brad quickly grabbed two corn
muffins, put them on a plate and placed it on
Rhonda's desk, and then he stepped back into the
safety zone.

"Well, you've got him trained," I said as I
took my place at the computer. Argus curled up
under my desk and sighed.

"What's new with you?" she asked.

"Same old, same old," I answered. "Oh, and
someone tried to burn my garage down last night."

"What?" screamed Rhonda. So I told her
about the last night's adventures. "Now I'm getting
worried about you."

"I'm sure it's just kids playing a prank," I told
her. I didn't really believe it, but I knew Rhonda
would overreact if she thought someone was really
out to get me. And truthfully, I wasn't at all sure that
anything that has happened is at all connected.

Before Rhonda could say anything Jackson
Bennett poked his head into the office and any

thoughts Rhonda may have had about my safety went out the window.

"Jackson!" she screamed. "What are you doing here so early?"

"I came to take you to lunch," he said.

"But it's only ten-thirty."

"I thought we could take a drive to Portland, and eat somewhere overlooking the harbor."

"I'll get my purse. Jesse, you and Brad are in charge until I get back."

"Since when do you carry a purse?" I asked.

"Wise ass," she answered as she drifted out of the store on Jackson's arm.

The rest of the morning I worked on the mail orders. At noon I sent Brad away for lunch and took over for him in the front of the shop. Business had been brisk earlier when a tour bus dropped off a group of visitors for an hour of shopping in the city. Oh yes, Bath is a city; it is a very small city, but it does have a city government. This, I'm sure, is a nod to the very powerful Bath Iron Works that is spread over much of the south end riverfront.

"Hi Jesse," said a voice. I looked up to see a middle-aged woman in a dark business suit and oversized red framed glasses standing in the middle of Erebus. There was something vaguely familiar about her, but I couldn't place it.

"Oh, hi" I said in a non-committal way.

"I hope I haven't changed that much Jesse," she said. "It's me, Monica, as in Monica Ashworth-Twist, you know, your cousin."

"Oh, my God! Monica! I haven't seen you since your wedding." I rushed over to give her a hug. "That was in 1974 when you married Jerry Twist

147

and moved to Georgia. Where the hell have you been?"

"I've been in Atlanta having a hell of a time helping Jerry with his dental office. Life goes by fast."

"How did you find me? Where are you staying? What are you doing here?" The questions just jumped out of my mouth.

"Hold on!" she laughed! "I'm staying at the Holiday Inn. I came to invite you to dinner. Then we can get caught up!"

"Great, I'll pick you up at seven and we'll go to Ruby's."

"Okay, I'll see you then" She waved at me as she went out the door.

"What the hell is this all about?" I said aloud to the empty store.

. . . .

Monica Ashworth-Twist and I practically grew up together. Her father and my father were brothers and her family lived about fifty miles away in Rockport. We were the same age, so at family gatherings we were always thrown together. Being related didn't mean that we liked each other; it was more a convenient teaming of us against the adults. We did share one thing in common and that was our grandmother Daisy. It was she who was the spiritualist and took every opportunity to teach us about the unseen world, much against both our parents' wishes.

I wasn't sure if Monica had developed her sixth sense since Grandma Daisy died or not. I was torn between my very rational mind that rejected other worldly experiences and my experiential world that relied on a very strong sixth sense to get by. Mostly, I didn't think about it much. If I often know things before they happen, so what? There is always a logical explanation; at least, that's what I tell myself.

When Rhonda returned I left for the day and headed home. I would check on Jason and then do some work on the cookbook before my dinner with Monica.

Jason was up and watching TV when I got home.

"Feeling better?" I asked.

"I'm feeling much better. My son called me and he's flying in tomorrow and staying for a week. I'll be out of your hair."

"I'm glad you're feeling better and you know you can stay here as long as you need to," I said.

"I know, but you know what they say, 'there's no place like home!'"

I left Jason to watch TV, fed Argus, and took him out in the back yard. Then I settled down to work on my cookbook. Using the editorial guidelines that Rhonda's sister sent me I figured I had about six hours of work left, if I worked quickly and efficiently. I had all the recipes lined up. All I had to do was write introductions or comments.

The problem I have with working with recipes is that I really begin to get hungry and want to go into the kitchen and cook up something. I had to remind myself that it really was too hot to cook and that the beef stew and biscuits would have to wait for fall. Thinking about food reminded me that I needed to lose about five pounds and that I should be working out more. Since my life had become busier, I'd been skipping the gym.

I was researching a recipe for "Bubble and Squeak" when the phone rang. I got up to answer the phone. "Hello," I said, but there was no answer, but in the background I could hear what sounded like the honking of a car horn, and then I heard a click. This was the third hang-up this week. It was, after all a relatively new number, so it was understandable.

I was so busy working on the cookbook that I lost all sense of time. When I finally looked at the kitchen clock it was time to go pick up my cousin at the Holiday Inn. I went to the refrigerator and put a plate of food together for Jason. I left Argus cuddled up with Jason in front of the TV and drove off to the Holiday Inn.

I had to cross the old Leeman Highway to get to the hotel, and the traffic was very heavy with tourists. As long as I could remember our license plates had "Vacationland" as a motto, and the traffic on route one was as much proof as anyone needed to the truth of the motto.

I arrived at the lobby just as Monica appeared. "Good timing," I said.

"Goodness has nothing to do with it," replied Monica in her best Mae West imitation. She and I used to watch old Mae West movies at family get-togethers. We both laughed.

"Are you ready?" I asked.

"We could eat here. They have a nice restaurant and it's not too busy for a Saturday night.

"It's fine with me." We entered the restaurant and were seated and placed our drink orders. In due course the drinks arrived.

"So tell me, Monica," I began as I gave her my best serious look. "Why are you here? We've only exchanged Christmas and birthday cards over the years, and then not every year, and now you show up out of the blue. Something is up! What's going on?"

Monica took a big sip of her martini. "I left my husband about two month ago, just as soon as the last kid was out the door. Jerry Twist is the biggest asshole in the state of Georgia, and that's really saying something. I needed to get away from the south and I thought of coming home to Maine. Then I had the awful feeling that you were in trouble and so I had to come and see you."

"How did you find me?"

"I've been keeping in touch with your parents, Uncle Clyde and Aunt Bonnie. They've kept me updated on you."

"And what trouble do you think I'm in?" I asked.

"Just that gut feeling Grandma Daisy always told us to pay attention to. And the fact that a body turned up buried in your yard, according to your mother. Now, you want to tell me what you've been up to or not?" Monica asked.

What the hell? I filled her in on my life to date, leaving out some of the details, but hitting on the major points. She was familiar with some of it because my mother kept her informed, but most of my life since moving to Bath she didn't know about.

"Holy Shit!" was her comment when I'd finished. "You do not lead a boring life do you?"

"I guess not, now that I listen to myself. In fact this has been a very busy summer and tomorrow is only the beginning of August." Our dinners arrived and we were silent for a while before either of us spoke again.

"So, Jesse, here's the big question. How do you really feel about all the stuff our grandmother believed in?"

I thought for a moment before speaking. How did I really feel?

"Well, sometimes I think it's all hooey, and sometimes I think there might be something in it. Mostly I don't think about it. How do you feel?"

"Mostly the same, except every once in a while I'll have a flash of insight or intuition and I can feel grandma nearby nodding at me," Monica answered.

"Funny, I feel the same way. She really did a number on us. Remember how mad our parents were when they found out she took us to the spiritual camp up in Northport?"

"Actually it was all very much forbidden and hence, a lot of fun."

Just then the lights in the restaurant dimmed for a few seconds and came back on.

"She's here!" whispered Monica and we both laughed.

Chapter 20

It was the first Sunday in August and the weather was perfect. It was also communion Sunday at church. I had cooked up some sausages and French toast and Tim, Jason, and I were sitting at the table finishing up our second cup of coffee. Jason was going to church with us, and it was to be his first venture out since he was shot. His son was arriving later in the day to pick him up and take him home.

"You're looking much better Jason," remarked Tim.

"Yes, I'm pretty tough for fifty-two," said Jason.

"Liar! You're fifty-six or more and you know it!" I put it.

"Bastard!" said Jason.

"Nice talk you two," said Tim with a roll of his eyes. "And on Sunday, too"

"By the way," I said to change the subject, "I invited my cousin Monica to come to church this morning, so she might show up."

"You have a cousin?" asked Jason. "And she's a woman? Is she married"?

"Actually, she just got divorced and is moving up here." Jason and Monica? It might work, I thought. "Though, I'm not sure she into middle-age giants."

"You are bad!" Tim said to me. "Let's go to church before you two burn in hell."

I put Argus in his crate, since I couldn't take him to church, even though he is much better behaved than some kids I've seen.

There's something about church in the summer. The scented breeze comes in through the open windows and the doors are open to the street. There isn't that closed in feeling that happens in the middle of winter when the inside air is stale and the nooks and crannies of old churches are drafty and cold.

The historic colonial church faces the park by the city library and always attracts visitors to the summer services. Today the church seemed comfortably filled. Rhonda and Jackson were already seated in the pews when the three of us arrived. Bill and Becky Simpson were the ushers for this Sunday and John and Dorothy Lowell were the door greeters. Monica walked in right after us and I introduced her to Tim and Jason and made sure she sat next to Jason. The music this Sunday was traditional and we opened with "A Mighty Fortress is Our God" as the processional hymn. I never realized what a great voice Tim had. The readings and the sermon all dealt with the theme of "who is my neighbor."

Communion was served to us in the pews using one of the antique communion sets from the church's collection. The shiny, ornate communion service stood in contrast to the very plain and unadorned sanctuary of the church. I sat there and it suddenly hit me that this was a new life. Six months ago I was teaching in New Hampshire and had a pretty settled life. Yet, here I am in a new place feeling completely at home. I wasn't among strangers anymore, but among friends. I guess that's what communion is for, to help you make connections with others. I sat back and gave a silent prayer of thanks. The Reverend Mary Bailey gave the benediction and we all left the church for lemonade and fellowship on the front lawn.

It was much too nice a day for people to linger after church, so after a quick glass of lemonade and a few words of greeting, everyone left to enjoy the day. Monica offered to drive Jason back to his house and wait for his son to show up. Rhonda and Jackson planned to go on a picnic, and Tim and I were planning to go back to Eagle's' Nest and work on the Helga case.

When Tim and I arrived at Eagle's Nest, Argus was more than ready to get out of his crate. Tim took him outside to do his business and I retrieved my note cards and put them on the kitchen table. I opened a can of Moxie for myself and a bottle of Pepsi for Tim. When Tim returned with Argus, we sat at the kitchen table, with Argus at our feet. I picked up the pile of note cards and tossed them to Tim.

"Here you go!" I said as I tossed the pile to Tim. He began placing them one by one on the table.

"Anything attract your attention on these?" he asked.

"Let's review them one by one," I suggested.

"Well, the last time we did this we never finished looking at them. Instead we went off to see old lady LaFond. But we've added a few more things since then," I said.

"Yes, someone shot Jason," Tim replied. "I think we should concentrate on what we don't know."

"All right then, we don't know who shot Jason. We don't know who set my garage on fire. And we don't know who Rita Toliver is and if she stole the dental records," and I added, "We don't even know if these events are related or not."

"Then," added Tim, "We don't know who left you the MYOB note or the phone calls."

"We still need to question the Turcotte sisters, if we can find them," I added. "And don't forget that Judy is Drone's half sister, which she's never mentioned, or that we have a picture of her in high school wearing the same type of peace medallion."

"I think it's time," began Tim, "to have an official talk with Bitch Blair. May I use your phone?"

"May I? Since when are you so grammatically correct?"

"Since I've been hanging with an English teacher."

"Smart ass!" Tim went into my guest room / office to use the phone. I looked at the cards and then flipped them over is frustration. I stared at the back of the cards and then picked one up. It read Rita Toliver. I turned it back over, shuffled the cards, and then picked one up again.

"What the hell!" I said aloud. I had turned over the same Rita Toliver card. My subconscious mind was sending a hint. Now what do I do with it?

I could hear Tim talking on the phone and then he hung up and came back in the kitchen.

"Something smells good in here."

"It's beef burgundy in the crock pot."

"Yum! I was on the phone with Bitch Blair. She agreed to come in tomorrow for questioning."

"She did? I find that hard to believe."

"Well," Tim hesitated. "She may have gotten the impression that it was more of a social request than an official one."

I laughed. "So what is the official status of the investigation?"

"Which one? There really are two. Helga's death and Jason's shooting. Jason's is still ongoing. I have an investigator questioning neighbors and friends, but officially it looks like a random attack. Helga's death is open but not active. The state is officially in charge of her case. Anything I do now is on my own time, and I have precious little of that, which is why I need your help."

"You need my help?" I asked.

"Of course we are a team, of sorts."

"Not to mention a few fringe benefits," I added.

"There is that," answered Tim with a smile.

Chapter 21

It was Monday morning and another beautiful August day. I was up early and had coffee on the back porch. Argus was sitting watching the birds fly around the back yard. All the day lilies I had planted were in bloom and everything looked lush and colorful. I was amazed at the transformation that had taken place in just seven weeks. The house and yard bore little resemblance to the old unpainted, abandoned looking cottage and the overgrown, weed infested yard I bought in the early spring.

I spent two hours working in the yard before it became too warm. For the rest of the morning I worked on my cookbook manuscript. I double checked everything, made sure it was all in order. Then I placed it into and envelope to be mailed to Rhonda's book-agent sister in New York. After that it was all up to her to find a publisher or not. I would put it out of my mind once the manuscript was in the mail.

Tim had asked me to sit in on his questioning of Judy Blair. It would be under the guise of lunch at Ruby's. I would meet them there at noon.

I put Argus in his crate, grabbed my package, and headed out the door. Since it was hot and the post office and Ruby's were in two different directions, I took the car. I hadn't driven in a few days and it was nice to be behind the wheel. As much as I like to walk, cars are faster and much easier on the feet.

I passed the manuscript to the post office clerk, who weighed it, place the appropriate postage on it, and threw it in a bin of outgoing mail. It was a relief to send it off. I felt like I had accomplished something, even if nothing ever became of it.

When I arrived at Ruby's Tim and Judy were already seated. I sat down at the table and got a dirty look from Judy.

"I asked Jesse to join us," Tim said to Judy. "I hope you don't mind?"

"Of course not," replied Judy with clenched teeth. If looks could kill I'd be lying on the floor with vultures tearing at my eyeballs "How are you Jesse?"

"I'm great Judy. Everything is going well!" I smiled.

"Super duper," She replied. The waiter came over and we gave him our orders.

"So Judy," began Tim. "Tell us about your half brother Richard Drone. I never even knew you had a half brother."

The smile on Judy's lips froze in place. She turned visibly pale, and her eyes got very wide. It took her a moment to recover her composure. We had hit on something, but I wasn't sure what it was. Our drinks arrived. Judy took a sip of white wine. I had a beer, and Tim had club soda because he was on duty. It was a few moments before she started speaking.

"He is my older brother, or rather half brother. My mother was married once before she met my father. Drone is ten years older than me so we didn't really grow up together."

"And," interrupted Tim, "you didn't bother to tell anyone that Drone lived in the Sagamore Street house around the same time that Helga was buried in the backyard?"

"I never really thought of it that way," stammered Judy.

"Bullshit!" I said. "You could have mentioned it when we had lunch in Portland. You figured out then that it was my house."

Just then the waiter arrived with our food, giving everyone a break from the intensity. I took a bite of my burger then continued:

"What about the medallion I found in the backyard. You wore one just like it in high school. The picture of us all was in the Press Herald, and you were wearing it in that photo."

Judy took a bite of her salad. "I don't remember that medallion. I don't know anything about Helga's death, and I'm sure my brother had nothing to do with it."

"Where is he now?" asked Tim.

"He lives in Stonington and builds wooden boats by hand."

"Why do you think he had nothing to do with her death?" I asked. "He was living there."

"He was the ultimate hippy. He believed in non-violence and was usually too stoned to get upset about anything."

"So, just to recap," I began. "You don't remember anything about the peace medallion and you don't think your brother had anything to do with Helga's death and burial in the backyard?"

"I don't remember the medallion and I don't have it now. My brother moved out of that house around the time we graduated, so he might not have even lived there then. And," Judy added, "This was all a long, long time ago."

We finished our lunch with very stilted small talk. Judy tried to flirt with Tim, but Tim pretended not to notice. As soon as Judy could, she excused herself and said she had to get back her business in Portland.

"She's hiding something," I said to Tim as soon as she left.

"You got that right. At least we have a line on Drone now."

"That we do."

One my way back home I parked on Front Street and went in to Erebus to tell Rhonda I had finished the cookbook, and that I had mailed it off to her sister.

"This calls for a celebration," she said. She went to the back room, got two glasses and took out some ice cubes from the freezer. She poured some bourbon in each glass and handed it to me.

"What did Tim say when you told him?" she asked.

"Actually, I didn't get a chance." Then I told her about lunch with Judy.

"Well, she sounds like a real bitch."

"Real enough," I replied.

The next morning was as clear and bright as the morning before. If summer was slipping away I didn't notice it. I wasn't feeling the countdown to Labor Day and the end of summer as I usually did. There would be no first day of school this year, no school calendar, no school bells. It was a refreshing and rather freeing feeling.

Argus was scampering behind me as I made an inspection of the back yard. The wildflowers I had planted over the crime scene were in bloom, but it still gave me an uneasy feeling. There were small green apples growing on an ancient apple tree in the further corner of the yard. I spent some time with a pair of clippers and pruned some of the rose bushes and trees. I should be inside fixing and cleaning the house, but it was too nice to be inside. The house would have to wait for fall.

I heard the phone ringing as I was heading back to the house. I knew the machine would pick it up. It also reminded me that I needed to check out the machine and see if I could figure out why it didn't record Jason's message. What other messages was I missing I wondered? I did have one message on the machine from Tim, which I had played back but not yet erased. So it was recording sometimes at least.

As I entered the kitchen I heard the machine click on:

"There's no one available to take your call. Please leave a message after the beep." It was my voice on the message. I waited to hear who it was before I picked it up. Instead of a message there was a series of three beeps and then I heard Tim's message replayed:

"Hi Jesse, it's Tim. Give me a call at the office when you have a chance."

Another beep and then the machine said in a very mechanical voice, "All messages have been erased." Someone had my answer machine code and was checking my messages and erasing them! How did they get my code? I picked up my answer machine and there it was on a label on the bottom with the call in code. Whoever did this must have been in my house!

. . . .

Tim wasn't pleased when I told him that someone had been intercepting my phone calls. I gave him the number that appeared on my caller ID and he said he would check it out, but that it might be untraceable. He was working late and so I wouldn't see him until tomorrow. I hung up the phone and called Rhonda.

"Are you busy? Can you leave Brad in charge? I want to get away from here for a few hours."

"What's up?" asked Rhonda.

"I'll tell you when I pick you up. Be outside the shop in ten minutes."

After I hung up I unplugged the answer machine. At least nobody could be checking my messages now. I picked up Argus and put him in the car, drove to Erebus, and picked up Rhonda. I headed north over the millennium bridge and up route one. After a few minutes Rhonda looked at me, "What's going on?"

I told her about the phone messages. "I just felt a little claustrophobic and needed to get away for a few hours."

"Wow! I don't blame you. Can the call be traced?"

"Yes, but it appears to be a cell phone number, and they are hard to trace sometimes."

We drove along until we reached the traffic bottleneck in Wiscasset. The traffic was backed up about two miles as route one runs through the main street of the town and then onto a narrow bridge over the Sheepscott River. On the left side of the road

163

was a red shack with a line of people circled around it.

"What's that?" asked Rhonda.

"Red's Eats. It has the best lobster rolls in the state. We'll have to come up here for lunch sometime." Rhonda was not familiar with any part of Maine north or east of Bath.

"This is a nice little town." She said.

"Yes, too bad it's cursed with this bottleneck traffic." After we made it to the bridge the traffic was much better and we had smooth sailing until we reached Camden. The drive gave us a chance to catch up and talk. We had been busy in the last few weeks and usually had other people around us.

When I saw the traffic backup outside of Camden, I took several side streets to get to the harbor. I snagged a parking spot on Chestnut Street, put a leash on Argus, and we walked down Frye Street to the public landing on the harbor.

"This looks just like a movie set!" remarked Rhonda as she looked at the harbor. Many of the windjammers were in and the harbor was filled with masts of sailing ships. In the background was Mt Battie. The combination of mountains and sea was dramatic. There was a general hustle and bustle of a working harbor going on. Argus was sniffing all the nice new smells.

"Over there," I pointed to a large windjammer with reddish sails, "is the *Doris Dean*. I worked as the cook on there for part of the summer back in '99. I've sailed three times since then." I saw a familiar shape emerging from cabin. "Let's go over and have a closer look."

I led the way to the head of the harbor, down the ramp to a series of floats. We paused next to the ship.

"Hey, Jeff!" I yelled to guy bending over a pile of ropes on the deck.

"Jesse! What the hell are you doing here?" Jeff Hardy is the tall, middle-aged captain and owner of the *Doris Dean*. He is also a distant relation of mine, as is, I imagine, half the people in the state. I was on a four-day cruise one summer when the temperamental cook walked out. I offered to take up the cooking for the last two days of the voyage. To my surprise I was asked to finish out the summer season as the ship's cook. It was hard work, but it was a great way to meet people.

"I'm just up for the day. This is my friend and former co-worker Rhonda Shepard. Rhonda, this is Captain Hardy." I made the introductions.

"Come aboard. The guests aren't arriving for another two hours." He turned to Rhonda, "Let me give you the tour." He helped Rhonda up the three steps to the deck as I carried Argus.

"This is Argus," I said as I sat him down on the deck.

"Good size dog for a ship like this," said Jeff as we stepped down into the ship. "Parker's not here. He said he had a dinner date; he's due back before six." Parker Reed is the first mate. He and I struck up a friendship when I was the cook. I had come back as a passenger several times in the past few years. "This is the main cabin where we can gather in bad weather. Over this way are the guest cabins."

"My, they are small," remarked Rhonda as she peeked inside. There were two bunks, a couple of coat hooks, and a washbasin with running water.

"When you've got the wind in your hair and the beauty of the Maine coast to look at, you don't spend much time in your cabin."

"And if I remember correctly, with the fresh air and the sunshine, most people turn in early and sleep like logs." I added.

"That they do. Let's go check out the galley," Jeff suggested.

"That will be a short tour," I said.

We stepped down a few steps and had to duck our heads to enter the galley, which was in the bow of the ship.

"You actually cooked here, Jesse?" asked Rhonda. There was a small wood stove, a double sink, a food locker, and a big scrubbed pine table. Everywhere there were pots and pans hanging from hooks. On the opposite wall was a big dish cabinet for all the dishes and silverware. In the bow were two curtained cubicles, which were bunks for the cook and crew. "How many people make up the crew and passengers?"

"About twelve on most voyages," answered Jeff.

"That's a lot to cook for. How did you do it, Jesse?"

"See that notebook over there?" I said as I pointed to a red binder on a small shelf. "That's a cook's log. All the cooks leave shopping lists, recipes, and comments. All I had to do was look through it and find what I needed. I even left some recipes there."

Rhonda was impressed with the ship, and I suggested that she take a cruise in the early fall and experience the coast when the leaves begin to change.

"Parker will be sorry to have missed you," said Jeff.

"I live in Bath now so I'll be stopping by again. Tell him I said 'Hi.'"

When we finished the tour we headed back to the public landing. We chose an outdoor restaurant on the wharf for dinner. It was getting dark when we were finally seated. Argus took his place under the table and was watching the seagulls that were boldly walking along the wharf. Despite the great summer weather the days were getting noticeably shorter. The sun was setting in the west and the red glow was reflected in the calm waters of Camden harbor.

"Thank you for bringing me here. I've been so busy this summer at Erebus I haven't had any time to explore," said Rhonda once our drinks arrived.

"Thanks for coming. I really needed to get away. I can't make any sense out of anything that's happening."

"I'm sure it will all sort itself out, or maybe even all go away. It is spooky that someone's been checking your voice mail, though."

"Well, at least retirement hasn't been dull. Remember all those endless homeroom periods and non-teaching duties we had to endure for all those years? Cafeteria duty was my all time favorite!"

"Not to mention," added Rhonda, "the antics of the Amazing Asshole."

"To retirement!" I said by way of a toast. We clinked our glasses together and watched the light in the sky fade away. I turned to look at the harbor and over my shoulder I saw Parker Reed sitting at a table in the corner. When he looked up, he recognized me and waved. I waved back and got up to say hi. I excused myself from Rhonda and headed to his table. His dinner companion was seated with his back to me, but there was something familiar about the set of the shoulders.

Parker got up and gave me a hug. "Jesse this is my friend Billy."

"Nice to meet you, Billy…" I started to say. The words died on my tongue because when he turned around I was face to face with Bill Simpson, minus wife Becky.

Stephen E. Stanley

Chapter 22

The phone rang, I picked it up and heard Tim say "You're not going to believe this one.

"Okay, what?" I asked.

"We were able to trace the phone number. It turned out to be one of those pre-paid cell phones, and you don't have to register to use it, just buy a calling card with cash and go online to activate the phone."

"So we don't know to whom the phone belongs?"

"Do you always talk like an English teacher?"

"I am an English teacher, remember?"

"Retired English teacher, remember? Anyway, here is the strange part. Whoever activated the phone did register it and you are not going to believe the name."

This was getting interesting. "What's the name?" I asked.

"Rita Toliver!"

"Oh my god! The same person who most likely took Helga's dental files from the storage facility."

"Yes, it's the first break we've had in this case."

"But it doesn't tell us anything," I said. "We don't know who Rita Toliver is or where to find her."

"But," countered Tim. "It does tell us that some of the stuff that's happening to you is related to Helga's death. And that's more than we've had before."

"Oh, I guess it does!" Sometimes I think I'm a little slow on the uptake. "So how did this Rita Toliver get my answer machine code?"

"Give me the brand and the model number of your machine and I'll have my computer whiz, officer Murphy, check it out."

I picked up my answer machine and gave him the information. "Do you think she could have been here in my house?"

"That's what we need to find out," said Tim.

We talked for a few more minutes. Tim was going to be away for a few days to take his daughter Jessica up to the University for Freshman Orientation. It was time to do a little housework. I could count on filling up one vacuum cleaner bag with dog hair, not to mention dust, dirt, and pollen.

When I finished dusting and vacuuming, I gave Jason a call to see how he was doing. I was surprised when Monica Ashworth-Twist answered the phone. I recognized her voice right away.

"Hi Monica, I must have dialed the wrong number. I was calling Jason." I joked. Let her explain herself.

"Very funny! I'm just over here visiting Jason. He seems really sweet and he's not bad looking either." Well, this is interesting!

"I take it he's not in the room then?"

"No, he's taking a nap, but he is doing much better. He's up and around and out of pain. But he tires easily."

"Well, if you don't have other plans, come for dinner around six tonight and bring Jason."

It was too hot to use the oven, so I went to the kitchen and dug out my crock-pot. I took four large chicken breasts, placed them between wax paper and pounded them flat. Then I placed a slice of ham and a slice of Swiss cheese on each breast and rolled them up and secured them with a toothpick. I placed them in the crock-pot and covered them with condensed mushroom soup. Dinner would be ready later and I wouldn't have to heat up the house. White trash cooking is great on busy days.

I harnessed up Argus and we headed off to Erebus. I was glad to have a part time job, not only for the extra money, but to get me out of the house a couple of days a week. It also gave me the opportunity to interact with people. Left to my own devices I think I would become a hermit, only going into town once a month to get supplies.

It was a warm, but dry day with a slight breeze. Again one of those perfect summer days when the air smells sweet and the sky is clear. Argus had to stop to smell and left his leg every once in a while, but we finally made it to the store.

Rhonda was managing the front of the store and Brad was in back unloading some new arrivals. I invited her to dinner to make up a table of four for tonight. I also asked her if she wanted to bring Jackson along, but she said he was working late.

"That crazy woman was here looking for you," said Rhonda.

"You'll have to be more specific," I replied. "All the women I know are crazy."

"You know, that one that's half of that boring married couple you inflicted on us."

"Becky Simpson?" I asked.

"That's the one. She came in here wearing one of those denim jumpers with a knit turtleneck and long sleeves. It must be eighty out and she dresses like that. You know I never trust a woman who dresses like that. And she had on plastic flip-flops! Can you believe it?"

"Oh, my god! You mean the fashion police didn't arrest her?"

"Joke if you want, but I'm telling you she's not all there!"

"Did she say what she wanted?"

"She said she just popped in to say hello."

"Strange," I said. Just then a customer walked into the store, so I went into the back room and started up the computer. There were quite a few orders that I had to fill. Business on the web was getting much better for Erebus. After I finished with the orders, I decided to do an Internet search on Rita Toliver, just to see what I would come up with. There were quite a few hits and I decided to check them out later. It was time to head home. I gathered up Argus and we headed back to Eagle's Nest. The walk gave me time to think. There were pieces of the puzzle everywhere, but I had the feeling that I was looking at something and not seeing it. The little voice in my head was whispering something to me, but I couldn't quite hear it.

I was in the middle of making my two-minute key lime pie for tonight's dessert, when the phone rang. I was going to let the machine pick it up when I remembered that I had unhooked it. I would have to get a new one soon.

"Hello," I said into the receiver.

"Hi, Jesse, it's Becky, how are you?"

"Oh hi Becky, just fine thanks for asking."

"I stopped by Erebus, but you weren't working."

"No, I usually go in late morning." Where was this conversation going?

"Bill and I were just wondering how you are settling in. It must be tough moving at your age." My age? Bitch!

"Not so tough. I grew up here remember?" What the hell! I thought.

"Well, finding a body in your backyard wasn't a good start. By the way anything new about that?"

"Nothing at all. I don't think it will ever be solved." So she was looking for gossip.

"And how is Jason? I just sent him a get-well card."

"I think he's going to be fine. He just needs to rest up and heal."

"Any idea who shot him?" she asked.

"None at all." I didn't have any gossip for her and was getting tired of the conversation. "By the way, how is Bill? I asked, remembering that the last time I saw him he was touching knees with Parker Reed. I wondered if he told her I ran into him, or not.

"Well, they keep him pretty busy. Overtime and double shifts and all."

"I see," I said. I saw very clearly as a matter of fact, but it was none of my business.

"Okay, well I just wanted you to know that Bill and I were thinking of you. You'll have to come to dinner again soon," she said before she hung up. I would need a good reason before I'd go back and visit Bill and Becky.

Rhonda was the first to arrive for dinner, so I made her the bartender. We both had a gin and tonic before Monica and Jason arrived.

It was plain to see when Jason arrived with Monica that they were taken with each other. I wasn't sure how long Jason had been divorced, but I knew that Monica's divorce wasn't legally final yet. I hoped they weren't jumping in too soon, but it really was none of my business. Still, I thought, I'll take it up with her the next time we talk alone.

Argus is always happy when I have visitors because it gives him more laps to sit in and more attention. Pugs are pack dogs and always happy with a crowd. People who don't like dogs don't come to my house. Argus was sitting under the table while we were eating and talking.

"…so that's pretty much all we know," I had just finished telling them about someone listening to and deleting my answer machine messages.

"Wow, this is all very surreal," said Jason.

"Jesse and I grew up in a very surreal family," said Monica with wink to Jason.

"So it seems to me that the whole key to this is Rita Toliver, whoever she is," added Rhonda.

"That's what I think," I said. "But I've no idea how to find out who she is, or where she is, or what her part is in all this."

"What's Tim say about all this?" asked Monica.

"Not much. He is concerned, but he has other things to do at work, so we are just working on it in our spare time."

"I never thought of you," observed Rhonda, "as a "we" type of person."

"I can be a "we" person," I said defending myself.

"No you can't!" replied Rhonda. "I've known you for over thirty years, and you are not a 'we' person."

I was about to say "We this!" and make a rude gesture to Rhonda when Monica spoke up, "What are you planning to do next?"

"I'm not really sure. I guess I'll just see how things work out," I answered.

"Be careful," replied Monica and then quickly covered her mouth like she hadn't planned to say anything out loud. She did give me a "we'll talk later" look, however.

The rest of the evening went quickly. Monica and Jason were curious about our lives as New Hampshire schoolteachers and we had plenty to tell. Monica talked about life as a northerner living in Georgia, and Jason talked about living your life in a town where you grew up. It seemed that we had come up with a theme for the evening. I noticed that Jason and Monica were sitting about as close to each other as they could get. It was about ten o'clock before we called it a night.

When everyone had gone home and the dishwasher was loaded, Argus and I sat on the back porch and listened to the sounds of night. The crickets were chirping and somewhere off in the trees I could hear the hooting of an owl. The stars were bright overhead, and I realized that I was no longer living in the city, cut off from nature, but here I had the best of both worlds. I was only a street away from the village and yet had a great spot that was almost like being in the country.

When I looked at the transformation I had made in only a few months, I was amazed. I had hooked up with people I hadn't seen in thirty-odd years and it was like I had never left. Rhonda represented those years away, and amazingly enough she, too, was here and a part of it all. Sitting there on my back porch with my dog snoozing in my lap, I realized that I really was at home.

Chapter 23

Life had pretty much fallen into a routine. In the morning I had coffee on my front porch, read the paper, and then dressed for the day. Several days a week I went into town and worked at Erebus. On days I didn't go to Erebus, I worked in the garden or in the house. As I got settled I moved furniture around, changed the artwork on the walls, and tried to find the right look for the house. I lack that natural artistic streak that some people have naturally for interior decoration. I have to use rules, minimal furniture, big pieces of art on the wall, and the use of only three colors per room.

Tim and I would spend his days off together, but they were few and far between during the summer. Often he would stop by between shifts, and sometimes we would meet for lunch, sometimes for dinner.

When Tim came back from dropping his daughter off at freshman orientation, he called me with some news.

"We ran a check on your brand and model of answer machine. That brand has only three codes it issues for remote message checking. All three are available on the company's web site, so anybody could get it, and then try all three codes until they found the one that works," Tim informed me.

"But how would someone know the brand of answer machine unless they had been here?" I asked. It was time to buy another, more secure, answer machine.

"Good point!" Tim replied. "You want to take a day trip to Stonington tomorrow and try to track down Drone?"

"Sure," I answered. It was arranged that he would pick me up in the morning. I called Brad Watkins and asked him if he would stop in after work at Erebus and feed and walk Argus. It was too hot to take Argus, and you can never, ever, leave a dog in a hot car for even a few minutes.

As soon as I hung up the phone, it began to ring again. I looked at the caller ID and answered the phone.

"Hello, Jesse," said an elderly voice.

"Good morning, Mrs. LaFond," I replied. Why was Old Lady LaFond calling me?

"How did you know it was me?" she asked.

"Caller ID, it said the name of the home, and you are the only one I know there."

"Can you stop by?" she asked. "I was going through some of my things and I found something you might be interested in."

"Sure, I can be there in about an hour." Now she had my attention.

"Good, I'll be expecting you." Then she rang off.

I stopped to get gas on my way to the Sagadahoc Nursing Home. Gas prices had gone up in the last few days. I pulled my Prius up behind a big Ford SUV and got a dirty look from the driver. I filled my tank, took my receipt, and went on my way. The SUV guy was still filling up as I pulled passed him. I could see that his total had reached fifty bucks and was still pumping. I waved at him as I left.

Old Lady LaFond was waiting for me when I got to the nursing home.

"Good morning Mrs. LaFond," I said as I entered her room.

"Good morning Jesse," she replied. "I have something here you might be interested in seeing. I'm sure Timothy will be interested as well. I was looking through my box of letters and mementos when I saw it."

I took the postcard she was holding and looked at it. It was an old postcard from the Flamingo Hotel and Casino in Las Vegas. It was dated August 1970 and was from Helga Johanson. The message said simply: We are in Las Vegas now and then off to LA and then a plane home. Thanks for everything, Helga.

"Wow!" was the only thing I could think to say.

"Yes, I said she got on the bus. I know that the bus was on a cross-country trip and that I saw her get on it. I don't think she ever came back here," said Mrs. LaFond

"This just gets stranger and stranger," I said. "I'll run this by Tim, see what he thinks. Thanks for finding this."

"Let me know how this all turns out."

I said I would stay in touch. I spent some time visiting with her, but I was anxious to take the postcard and show Tim. After a cup of tea, I flew out the door and drove to the police department.

"Chief is in a meeting right now," said the officer at the desk.

"I'll wait." I told him.

"Anything I can help you with?" he asked.

"No, it's some information he might find interesting." The cop gave me one of those looks that cops have for crazy people who show up at police stations. I ignored it.

After a few minutes Tim came out of the office. "Jesse, why are you sitting out here?" he asked. The cop at the desk gave me a started look and quickly looked busy. Interesting!

"I thought you ought to see this," I handed him the postcard.

"Shit!" Tim said when he turned it over and read it. "How did you get this?"

I told him about the phone call and visit to Old Lady LaFond

"Well," said Tim when I finished telling the story, "She must have come back here at some point. The problem now is that we don't have a timeline for her death; all we have are more questions."

"You still want to go look for Drone tomorrow?" I asked.

"Sure. Maybe he can give us something to go on. Anything might help at this point. You free for dinner later?"

"You bet, stop by when you get off work." I could see the officer at the desk react to Tim's dinner offer. His eyes got wider as he tried to look busy. I don't think he would make a good poker player. I bet he couldn't wait to get to the water cooler with his officer buddies. As I walked out of the police station the officer at the desk gave me a nod.

The next morning I was up and dressed before Tim finished his shower. We decided to stop and have breakfast on the way to Stonington. The morning was foggy and cool, and I was pretty sure the fog would burn off later and that it would be a nice sunny day. I drove and we took the highway to Bangor, where we stopped for breakfast. Then we headed east to Blue Hill, through Penobscot and on to Deer Isle.

Stonington is the largest town on Deer Isle, but before you get on the island you have to drive over this really scary bridge. It's a very old, narrow suspension bridge with a steep incline in the middle. I always pray that I don't meet a truck halfway. After the bridge we headed over the winding causeway to the main island, again hoping to avoid an encounter with any trucks. Luck was with me and there was no other traffic.

Stonington lies on the further side of the island. It is the perfect little Maine fishing village and looks more like a movie set than an actual working harbor. Its remote location off the beaten track has kept both development and spoilage down. I parked the car on the main street, and we got out and headed to the boat shed where Richard Drone worked.

"I've lived in Maine my whole life," said Tim, "and I've never been here."

"It's a big state. I only know about it because my grandparents grew up here," I told him.

The boat shed was easy enough to find. It was a weathered wooden structure at the end of the harbor with a sign that read Drone's Wooden Boats. The doors were open and three men were working on the upside down hull of a large vessel. Two of the men appeared to be in their twenties and the third had long gray hair pulled back in a ponytail and appeared to be in his sixties. Using superior deduction skills we pegged the latter as Drone.

"Richard Drone?" The man nodded. "I'm Police Chief Tim Mallory of the Bath Police Department. Could we go somewhere and talk?"

"Sure. My office is right over there," the man replied. He led us to a small office with a desk and several wooden chairs. There were boat blueprints spread all over his desk. A fan on top of the file cabinet moved the warm, stuffy air around.

I introduced myself.

"I'm Jesse Ashworth. Tim and I graduated with your sister Judy, back in the day."

"Nice to meet you both. Now what is this about?"

Tim gave Drone the nickel version of the story, explaining that he was investigating the death of Helga Johanson and my interest in the case as the current owner of Eagle's Nest.

"I read about the case in the Bangor paper, but I really didn't connect it at all. The name didn't ring a bell with me, and there was no mention of the address where the body was found. The old lady and I lived in the house for about three years and moved out around the time my sister graduated. Lots of good dope back then, so I don't remember a lot," Drone laughed.

Tim took out an envelope and passed him a photo of Helga. Drone looked at it for a minute or two before he spoke.

"Yes, I remember her. She was foreign wasn't she?" he asked.

"Yes," I said. "She was an exchange student from Denmark."

"She used to show up at the house now and then, usually with some guy or other. She was a real looker. By the way," he said to Tim. "You used to come by once in a while too, didn't you?"

"I might have been there once or twice," Tim blushed. "Did she get along with everyone?" Tim asked. "Was she ever involved in any trouble?"

"No, not that I remember. I think she was on the quiet side. My old lady might remember more than me. You know how women are."

"Yes," Tim and I said at the same time.

Drone gave us directions to his house and called ahead to tell his wife Dusty to expect us.

"Do you think the name Dusty refers to her housekeeping skills?" I asked Tim when we were alone in the car.

"More likely an affinity for drugs," answered Tim.

"I hadn't thought of that."

"You wouldn't!"

We drove over the hilly island roads to the village of Sunset, half-way between Stonington and the town of Deer Isle. Drone and Dusty lived in an old farmhouse up a long gravel driveway. Much to my shock the house was as neat as a pin. It was an old cape style house with a fresh coat of white paint and newly painted green shutters. Day lilies were in bloom everywhere and pots of red geraniums lined the walkway to the house.

Dusty greeted us at the door. Rather than looking like an aged hippy, she was small and dressed in casual L.L Bean style pants and blouse. Her hair was short and neatly coiffed.

"Hi, you must be Tim," and she turned to me and added, "You must be Jesse." With Tim's size and manner, it wasn't hard to figure him as the cop. "Come in. I've just made a pot of coffee and some muffins."

She led us to the kitchen, which was as neat as it was comfortable. She poured us coffee and gave us each a muffin. They were blueberry and they were very good.

"I remember Helga, she was a nice girl. I think Judy brought her a few times and she came with some big guy on occasion, too."

"Jason?" I asked. He was a big guy and he admitted to being there.

Dusty thought for a minute. "Yes, I think that was the name."

"What can you tell us about Helga?" Tim asked.

"We girls always hung around together. We used to hang out in the kitchen away from the men. We talked a lot. I know Helga didn't have any family and was somewhat homesick. She loved hanging out with us, she said, because I remaindered her of some of the people she knew in Denmark. She hated all the politics of the war and all that was going on. It really depressed her. We tried to get her interested in protesting the war, but she didn't feel comfortable, since she was a guest in the country."

"Did she have any enemies?" I asked.

"Goodness, no! I think maybe some of the girls were jealous of her because the guys all liked her and she was so pretty. But I don't think anyone hated her enough to kill her."

"Your husband said you moved out of the house in June of the year Judy graduated. Is that correct?" I asked.

"He was fried! He wouldn't remember!" she laughed. "We both gave up drinking and drugs decades ago, by the way. We moved out in April of that year and moved here, you can check the town records."

"Do you know who lived in the house after you left?" I asked.

"Not really," she replied. "I think it was vacant for several months, but I'm not really sure why I remember that."

"Well, thanks for the coffee and muffins," Tim said to her. "You've been very helpful."

"No problem! Always glad to help out hometown people."

"Are you from Bath?" I asked.

"Morse High, class of '65" she replied.

"Tim and I were '70's graduates," I said as we got in the car. She waved as I backed the car down the driveway.

"You should have said, very early seventies," Tim said to me as we drove away.

It was lunchtime, so before heading back I drove us to Stonington for lunch at the Fisherman's Friend Restaurant. On the way into town I pointed out the house where my grandparents used to live.

We sat by the window and watched village life go by outside. I ordered the scallop stew, which is the best I've ever had anywhere at any time. Tim ordered the fried Maine shrimp.

"You seem to have a knack," Tim said to me between mouthfuls of food, "for finding the best restaurants any place you go."

"It's a gift," I said. "One among many that I possess."

"What other gifts do you have?" asked Tim, teasingly.

I leaned over the table and whispered my answer.

"True," said Tim and gave me a wicked smile.

After lunch we got in the car and headed back home. The traffic was light considering that it was the middle of the tourist season.

"So," I said as we eased off the Deer Isle Bridge onto the mainland, "if Helga got on that bus at the end of June, and Dusty and Drone had moved here two months earlier, then they probably had nothing to do with her death."

"It looks that way. In fact it sort of makes sense. If the house was vacant at the time, it would be easier to bury the body. You can, after all, see the back yard from your screen porch. So either no one was there at the time, or whoever was living there knew about the body," Tim answered.

We were both silent for a few miles. "We are never going to solve this, are we?" I asked.

"I think sooner or later someone is going to slip up. We just have to pay attention when it happens. Look at all that's happened since you moved back to Bath. Your snooping around has someone's attention."

"I guess you're right about that," I said as we drove along. I looked at the clock on my dashboard. "Time for a beer?"

"You got that right!" answered Tim.

Chapter 24

It was around nine in the morning and I was outside straightening out my tool shed when I heard the phone ring. I hadn't replaced my answer machine yet so I ran into the kitchen and answered the phone.

"Hi, Jesse. It's Janice," said Rhonda's sister on the other end. "I found a publisher for your cookbook!"

"You're kidding!" I couldn't believe it.

"No, they loved it. They want to change the order of the recipes and give it a different title, but other than that it's good to go. I'll FedEx the contracts to you."

"This is great!" I was excited. "What title do they want to use?"

There was a slight hesitation. "They want to call it White Trash Cooking," she answered in a forced happy voice.

"What?" I asked in disbelief. I often referred to myself as a white trash cook, but to have it in print was something else again.

"I think it's a great title," she said.

"Hey, I don't care if they call it Cooking with Poop at this point," I said after I gave it some thought.

"Good," Janice sounded relieved, "I've contacted Maynard White Photography in Portland to do your book jacket photo. We are going to move fast on this one, so I need you to set up an appointment today. He'll be expecting your call. You should get the contracts tomorrow. Look them over and sign them and FedEx them back ASAP."

"Will do," I answered. "I'm a little stunned. I really didn't think it would go anywhere."

"Well," said Janice, "You have a great agent. Talk to you later!"

As soon as she hung up the phone I called Rhonda. She screamed when I told her the news. "I knew you could do it. I'm going to sell copies here in the store and have you autograph them!"

Next I called Tim, my cousin Monica, and my parents in Florida. Everyone congratulated me, though I cautiously said that I would believe it when I saw it in print.

....

I am not," I said emphatically, "wearing that outfit in a photograph!" Maynard White was a smallish, sixty something man with a shiny, bald head and big, thick glasses. Not my idea of what a famous photographer should look like.

"But this is supposed to be a fun cookbook, so we need a fun photo for the book jacket." He handed me a pair of cut off blue jeans, a white t-shirt, black plastic flip flops and a paper short order cook's hat. "Your agent said to really camp it up."

"Fine," I said as I yanked the clothes out of his hand and stomped off to the dressing room.

"That looks great," said Maynard when I returned from the dressing room.

"Just so you know, I would never wear any of these things, and certainly I would never wear plastic flip flops!" I fumed.

"Of course not. Now let's get in the car and go on location."

189

"Location!" I wasn't amused. "You want me to go out in public like this? But this is a studio. Can't you take my picture here?"

"Oh no," he replied. "You look great. I want to get you outside for some local color."

I thought about how great I'd look sitting on the rocks at Portland Headlight, or at the top of the Portland Observatory. Maybe I could be looking off the stone bridge in Deering Oaks Park with a dreamy look in my eyes. Maybe some local color would make this horrible outfit not so bad. He was, after all, a highly regarded professional.

"Sure, local color, whatever," I said and we got in his car. We drove through Portland into the country, past a lake and up a dirt road.

"What the fuck is this?" I asked as I looked around in disbelief.

"Local color," replied Maynard. We had stopped in the middle of a trailer park. Not a nice mobile home park with green lawns, paved streets and retro street lights, but a run-down 1950's trailer park with rusted and abused trailers sitting on gravel lots.

Maynard got out of the car and started setting up his camera equipment. "We rented this unit for the day to get some good shots."

"The only good shots you are going to get will be if I can find a gun!" I yelled.

Maynard motioned me over to the faded blue trailer. "I want you to sit on the front steps. You are the white trash cook and this," he said as he waved his arm around the neighborhood, "is local color."

I sat on the steps while he clicked away with his camera. I was becoming less excited about being

190

published by the minute. Maybe nobody would look at the back of the book jacket. Finally he was done and I got up to go.

"Okay, now we need to get some inside shots," said Maynard smiling.

"You want me to go inside this thing?" I asked in horror.

"I want to get some shots of you cooking."

"I can't cook here!" I protested.

"You don't really have to cook, just look like you are cooking." Maynard said as he held the door open for me. I went up the steps and entered into the very small kitchen. The ceiling was so low my head almost touched it. Everything was paneled in a light plywood finish and the appliances where from the 1950's and they were pink!

"I can't be seen in a pink kitchen! People will lose their appetites!"

"Just grab that big pan, fill it with water, put it on the stove and stir it with that spoon," Maynard directed.

"I can't use this pan. It's aluminum!" My humiliation was complete, and I posed while Maynard clicked away. I just hope somebody, somewhere, knew what he or she was doing.

"You poor thing," said Rhonda, biting her lip to keep from laughing when I told her about my day. I guess it was funny now that I was telling her, but it didn't seem so at the time. We were seated in my kitchen eating a shepherd's pie I had made for dinner. Argus was under the table keeping watch for any falling crumbs.

"You made enough of this stuff to feed an army. What are you going to do with it all?"

"I'll send some home with you and freeze the rest." I often cooked large batches of food and filled the freezer. It was good for those days when I didn't feel like cooking.

"Good," said Rhonda. "I hate to cook."

"So what's up with you?" I asked. "I haven't seen you with Jackson for a while."

"He's away in California visiting with his kids for two weeks. He'll be back in a day or two."

"He has kids?"

"Two grown sons. One is in LA and the other in San Francisco."

"Wife?"

"Dead!"

"Okay, just checking," I said.

"What's for dessert?" asked Rhonda, changing the subject.

"Madeleine's," I said. I set down a plate of the buttery, shell-shaped cookies.

"Heaven," said Rhonda biting into one.

"Out with it, Rhonda, I know something is on your mind. Out with it."

"My relationship with Jackson needs a boost. I was thinking of booking a cruise for the two of us on the *Doris Dean*. I wanted to run it by you before I bring it up to him. Could you run the shop for a week?"

"I think that's a great idea. I'd be glad to run the shop. I'll call the captain as soon as you clear it with Jackson."

"You are a good friend."

"Don't get gushy on me," I said.

. . . .

Summer showed no signs of slowing down. The garden was blooming and the weather remained clear and warm. The smell of the early morning was sweet and clean, and I took Argus for a walk.

John Lowell was out puttering around his yard when Argus and I walked by. Dorothy was on the porch and invited me to sit for a cup of coffee. John left his puttering and came and joined us on the porch. Dorothy excused herself for a minute and came back with some homemade doughnuts. Argus sat on my lap hoping to get a few doughnut crumbs. We talked about the weather, and I got some of the political gossip about the local school board. Apparently school boards around the country were pretty much the same. I thought this would be a good opportunity to ask them about the neighborhood.

"Eagle's Nest," I said, "was in pretty bad shape when I bought it. How long had it been vacant?"

"I think," said Dorothy, looking at John for confirmation, "that it was vacant about a year and a half before you started to fix it up."

"That's right," agreed John. "Before that there was a family with four kids who lived there. Noisy bunch they were too."

"Chief Mallory and I tracked down the hippies who lived there in the seventies. They said the place was vacant for some time after they moved out. Do you remember that?" I asked.

John was silent for a moment before he spoke. "It was vacant for quite some time, though once we had to call the police because some local kids were using it as a party site. The owner died and it took a few years to settle the estate, and then it was sold and rented out again."

"We never bothered much with the renters," joined in Dorothy. "They only stayed for a year or two and then moved away. Nobody ever stayed for long."

"There was that one widow," said John, "who lived there for five or six years. She was friendly and nice enough."

Argus was getting restless and it was time to go. I finished my coffee and thanked them. I had learned something at any rate. I would ask Tim to check the police records about calls to Eagle's Nest for loud parties.

It was Saturday. I had lost track of the days and only realized it when Argus and I saw Bill Simpson out mowing his lawn.

"Hi, Jesse," greeted Bill. "Are you out walking the little gremlin?"

"I'm also trying to get my exercise. I used to ride my bike back in New Hampshire, but there are too many hills here."

"There's a great bike path in Brunswick. Becky rides there and I go jogging. Also Portland has a great recreation trail. You should try those."

"I've seen the one in Brunswick, I think. It runs along the river, right?"

"Yes that's the one."

"Good, I'll give it a try. I need to get back in shape. I haven't exercised much since moving back here. Where's Becky?" I asked.

"She's gone to the store. She should be back any minute." Now was a good time to escape then.

"Tell her I said hi. I should get going. I'm on my way to check on Jason." I wasn't really planning to visit Jason, but it made a great excuse to leave before Becky returned. Actually maybe I should check on Jason.

A cool sea breeze had just come up making the air quite refreshing. I checked Argus for signs of heat stress, but he seemed to be enjoying the walk so we continued to Jason's house on foot.

"Hey, Jason," I yelled through the open screen door.

"Come on in," Jason yelled back. I stepped into his small living room.

"How are you feeling?" I asked.

"Great, I'm going back to work tomorrow. I've had enough of sitting around. Plus I've used up too many sick days."

"That's what sick days are for."

"Getting shot in your front yard is very different from having the winter sniffles."

"You've got a point there," I observed.

"Ah," began Jason in a hesitant manner, "what do you think about your cousin?"

"Honestly? We were close growing up. After college we went our separate ways, as people tend to do. We kept in touch for major events, but that's been it until she showed up one day at Erebus. We were able to pretty much pick up where we left off. She's honest and a bit of a mystic. She inherited the family trait of well-tuned intuition. That's about all I can tell you. Are you guys serious?" I asked.

"Yes, I think we are serious. Why waste time at this point in our lives? I've been alone for too many years, and Monica has been in a bad marriage for too long. What about you and Tim?"

"That's a good question. We like being together and we like having some space. I think if we were both twenty, we would be moving in together and setting up housekeeping. Now, though we both have a life. Tim has his daughter and a career, and I'm just getting settled into retirement. Nothing seems urgent at this point."

We were silent for a time.

"Not to get too mushy," said Jason. "But I'm glad you're back. Thanks for helping me out and being a good friend, you total and complete asshole!"

"Up yours, you giant freak," I replied as we hugged and laughed.

Chapter 25

There was a chill in the August air. Summer was far from over, but the cool Canadian air mass that had settled over Maine was a reminder that fall was coming sooner rather than later. In response to the shorter days, the flowers were blooming in profusion, releasing their perfume in the early morning air. The morning glory seeds I had thrown in the backyard were now opening their blue blossoms to the morning sun. Argus was sniffing around the backyard as I was sitting on the back steps with my coffee, enjoying the morning air. Argus hates the heat, so he was rushing around with the energy that comes from the cool, bracing north wind.

It was a workday for me at Erebus, so I had a pan of banana muffins in the oven to take to work. Brad Watkins had the day off, so it would just be me and Rhonda at the store today. I expected to have a lot of on-line orders to fill when I got in.

Argus came running up to me and jumped up in my lap and began to lick my face. It meant that he was ready to start the day. I harnessed him up and we headed to town.

"What are you smiling about?" I asked Rhonda as I entered the shop. She looked like the proverbial cat that had swallowed an exceptionally big, fat canary.

"Jackson and I are going on the *Doris Dean* next week. He said yes and it's all arranged. That is if you don't mind working the store with Brad."

"Of course I don't mind! Good for you!"

"We had to do it as soon as possible because Brad will be going back to school in two weeks."

"Is he still going to work after school begins?" I asked.

"Oh. Yes, he said he loves working here. What's in the bag?"

It was a sign as to how excited she was about her cruise with Jackson. Any other day she would have noticed the bag of muffins first.

"Banana muffins," I said as I handed one to her.

"I hope the food is going to be good on the ship."

"The food is going to be outstanding. The sea air is going to heighten all your senses and the food is going to be like nothing else you've ever had." I promised.

"I can't wait."

"Well, I should get to the computer and check out the orders," I said as I headed into the back room.

It seemed to take forever for the computer to fire up, but once it was ready I received a dozen orders that needed filling. Ouija boards, tarot cards, crystals, and pentagrams seemed to be good business. Personally I wouldn't have a Ouija board in my house if you paid me, but given my spiritualist background, that wasn't surprising.

At first, I was so busy that I didn't see her standing in the doorway. When I looked up I saw Officer Jan Murphy waiting for me to finish my typing.

"Chief wants to see you," was all she said to me when I looked up.

"Sure," I said. "I can finish up here in about half an hour and be over there." I answered.

"He said he wants to see you," she said firmly, "now!"

"Did he say why?" I asked as I got up to go with her.

"No," she said. "I didn't ask. When he uses his chief's voice, you don't ask questions."

I nodded. I had been in the police station a few times and had heard his "chief's voice."

I stowed Argus with Rhonda and headed to the police station with officer Murphy. The statuesque blonde got more than a few looks from the men on the street, but if she noticed the looks at all she seemed not to react. I followed officer Murphy into the police station. She held the door to Tim's office open for me to enter, but she did not go in herself.

Tim was sitting at his desk with a grim look on his face. His hands were folded in front of him and he glanced up when I entered the room. Sitting in front of his desk was a rather plump woman with her back to me. She turned around when Tim looked up.

"Hello, Jesse," she said.

My knees began to buckle under me and my head was spinning. I reached for a chair against the wall to help steady me and I sat down. Though she was older and plumper than the last time I saw her, there was no mistaking her identity. It was Helga Johanson!

. . . .

After the initial shock had worn off, Helga told her story. Helga was a freelance travel writer living in New York City. She was married and had three grown children. After high school she had traveled around the country and decided to stay in California. Later she moved to New York and got married. Her married name was Benson, and she used Johanson-Benson as her professional name. She was in the habit of Googling her name every once in a while to see any mention of her travel articles on the Internet. When she stumbled across the story of her apparent death in an Internet search a few days ago, she decided to come to Bath in person to help straighten up the mistake.

"But we have your dental records," I said.

"I've been thinking a lot about that. I never went to the dentist when I was here. I think I might have an idea about that," stated Helga.

"Go ahead," said Tim. I noticed that he was taking notes as she was telling her story.

"Do you remember Brenda Wilson?" asked Helga.

"No, I can't say I do," I said.

Helga looked at Tim and he shook his head.

"And that was the big problem," replied Helga. "No one noticed Brenda. She was quiet and had no friends. She was an orphan and lived with a great aunt who was quite elderly. I liked Brenda, and I was about her only friend. She never had money for nice clothes and couldn't afford much of anything. She was in our class and all the rest of you ignored her like she wasn't there.

"She had a very painful toothache one day. I had an insurance policy for health and dental care that we foreign exchange students got for unexpected emergencies. I gave her my card so she could go to the dentist. I was sure no one would check too closely. I think that the dental records are those of Brenda Wilson."

As a teacher I was aware of what we now call the invisible child. The invisible child is a student who never speaks out or acts out, but turns in all his or her work and often gets overlooked in the classroom. Many of these students have few friends and in some cases are picked on outside of class. Now teachers have been trained to look for the invisible child, but I was sure back in the seventies a child like that would be ignored. Brenda Wilson must have been an invisible child. I certainly didn't remember her.

While I was thinking, I became aware that Tim was asking me a question.

"I'm sorry, I was thinking," I said to Tim.

"Yes, I could tell. I just asked you to keep this to yourself until I can get to the media. They are going to have a hay day with this."

"No problem," I replied.

"Thank you, Helga, for coming in person. And I might add, I'm very glad to see you among the living," said Tim.

"Yes," I added. "I'm glad to see you alive and well. One more question though. She was found with a polka dot dress that you wore in a photograph. Any idea how she got it?"

"I don't remember the dress, but I did give her some of my clothes before I left. I like to travel light."

"That's about all I can think of at the moment," I said to her.

"Where can I reach you if I have any more questions?" asked Tim.

Helga gave Tim one of her business cards.

"There's one more thing," said Helga as I got up to leave.

"Yes?" asked Tim.

"I know who killed Brenda,"

"Who?" asked Tim and I at the same time.

"Bitch Blair!"

Chapter 26

Bath is unique in small town design in that it seems to have two main streets. Front Street runs in front of city hall and contains much of the shopping area. Center Street runs perpendicular to Front Street, starting at city hall on one end and at the top of a hill, and seeming to end at the Sagadahoc Court House facing city hall at the top of another hill. In front of the courthouse is a small triangular park, which has a war memorial dedicated to the soldiers of past generations.

At the bottom of the hill, halfway between these two edifices is Water Street, where the police station is located. It was here that Tim Mallory and I sat staring at Helga Johanson

"What makes you think that Judy Blair killed Brenda Wilson?" asked Tim.

"Judy got a kick out of bullying Brenda. She did mean things to her all the time. Brenda was quiet and shy, and had no idea how to fight back. No one defended her. Brenda only had a few good clothes. One time Judy took ink and smeared it on one of Brenda's good dresses. Brenda started to cry and Judy made fun of her and started laughing. I was so mad I smacked the bitch and told her if she ever did something like that again, I'd kill her. She backed down for a while, but she was fuming. As soon as I left I bet she killed Brenda. And you," she said pointing at Tim accusingly, "You where Judy Blair's boyfriend. You should have stopped her!"

"I was not, in fact, her boyfriend," replied Tim. "And I knew nothing about any of this. Did you, Jesse?"

"No, I never knew any of this. Who else knew?" I asked Helga.

"I remember some of her cheerleader friends watched Judy. I really don't remember who else."

"Do you have any evidence that Judy Blair killed Brenda Wilson?" Tim had switched back to his police chief persona.

"No, but she was the only one who hated Brenda."

"Did Brenda have any boyfriends?" I asked.

"She said she was seeing someone in our class, but she wouldn't say who. She said they wanted to keep it a secret."

Tim and I asked a few more questions, but Helga didn't have any answers for us. She left and Tim and I just looked at each other for a few minutes.

"Wow!" I said.

'Wow! Doesn't even begin to describe it," said Tim.

"What now?"

"We try to confirm that the remains are indeed those of Brenda Wilson."

"There must be medical records somewhere. We all had physicals back in elementary school. Dr. Gallant, I think, was the school physician back then," I said.

"I think you're right, I'll check into it. Would you go back and check the yearbook and see if you can scan a picture of Brenda Wilson?" asked Tim.

"Sure will," I said as I got up to leave.

"And remember not to tell anybody about this yet until we can confirm something."

"Of course," I answered. Shit! Whenever I was told not to say anything, it just made me want to tell someone all the more!

I don't know about you, but when someone I think is dead suddenly appears alive and well, it sort of throws me off for a while. Not that it happened often, or ever for that matter, but I was having a hard time wrapping my mind around this.

I walked back to Erebus and told Rhonda that something important had come up and that I needed to go back home. I harnessed up Argus, and we headed back to Eagle's Nest.

It took me a few minutes to find the yearbook. Flipping through the book I found Brenda Wilson's picture. Funny thing is I thought I knew everyone in my class, but I didn't remember her at all. Looking through the book, I realized that there actually were several kids I didn't know. Was it possible that I never shared a class with them in all twelve years of school?

I scanned the yearbook photo and faxed it to Tim at the police station. Argus was following me around with that look I knew meant that it was time to do potty in the yard. Outside was cool and dry, and I pulled some weeds while Argus was sniffing around. I heard a strange sound and looked up into the sky to see the distinctive V formation of a flock of ducks heading south. Merrymeeting Bay, just northwest of Bath, was a migration point for waterfowl. Growing up in the area I had come to know the signs of the change in seasons.

Summer was slipping away and soon it would be the first day of school. This would be the first time since I was five years old that I hadn't gone to school after Labor Day.

When the mail came there was a very large envelope from my publisher's office. I opened it up and found the galley proofs. It was my job now to go through them and check for errors before the final printing. Who knew how much work a simple cookbook would be? I emailed Janice Shepard-Swanson, since she was my agent, in addition to being Rhonda's sister. I just wanted her to know that I was working on the galley proofs.

I still had no idea what the finished cookbook would look like. Janice said that the publisher would have some illustrations done by a food stylist. I just hoped the author's picture on the book jacket would be small. I still shuttered at the thought of me sitting on a trailer's steps in cut-off jeans!

I made a pot of coffee and settled on the front porch to go through the recipes, just to make sure that nothing was left out. Argus had settled down for a nap under my chair, when a Subaru with Maine plates pulled up in front of the house. Argus jumped on my lap for a better view. The car door opened and Parker Reed stepped out.

"Hey Parker! What's up?" I asked as he came up the walk. Parker was ten years younger than I. He was good looking and in-shape. He also liked older men.

"This place sure is hard to find."

"How did you find it?" I asked.

"Your friend at Erebus gave me directions. It's good to see you again, Jesse."

"Good to see you, too!" I wasn't sure why he was here, but I had a good idea.

"The last time I saw you, you were having dinner with Bill Simpson." I figured this might be the reason he was here.

"I didn't know he was married until you saw us in Camden. It was then that he told me. Now he's afraid that Becky will find out, and embarrassed to talk to you, so I said that since we had a history, I'd talk to you."

"You don't have to worry; I'm not in the habit of sticking my nose into people's private affairs. Besides, Becky is an idiot,' I said. "So whose midlife crisis is this? Yours or Bill's?"

"A little bit of both I guess," he answered.

"Do you think Becky knows anything?"

"Bill thinks she suspects something, but she doesn't know anything."

"Whatever," I said. "I know you didn't come here just to ask me to keep my mouth shut. You know me better than to think I gossip."

"I was hoping you could give me some background on Bill."

"I can tell you what I know, but you need to realize that there is a thirty-something year gap in my information. What do you want to know?" I asked.

"I want to know about his marriage. Do you think he likes guys or is this just a midlife experiment?"

"Well," I began. "Becky went after him in high school and pretty much ran the show then. I've been with them several times since I moved back here and she still seems to run things. She never really lets him out of her sight or even lets him have an opinion of his own. So I think his personal growth has been stunted. I also know that he experimented in high school." Was I blushing? "That's about it," I said.

"Well, thanks for sharing. This is a nice place you've got here," said Parker, changing the subject.

"Thanks! Come along, I'll give you the tour." We ended up in the kitchen sipping coffee.

"So are you glad to be back in Maine?" Parker asked.

"It was strange at first. I followed my friend Rhonda up here. Even though I grew up here it had been over thirty years since I had seen anyone from high school. I started running into people I knew, and it was like I had always known them. I found this house and fixed it up and it's beginning to seem like home."

"You've done a great job on the house. It looks like something from a magazine."

"Thanks, Parker," I said. Always good to hear compliments.

"Are you going to work the cruise next week? My friend Rhonda and her man-friend Jackson are going for the four day cruise on the *Doris Dean*."

"Yes, I'll be working. I'll take good care of them."

"You might want to make sure they have a private cabin. You know how thin the walls are on the ship," I said.

"Yes, if I remember right, you and I got applause when we appeared one morning," said parker laughing at the memory.

After Parker Reed left I decided to take a ride out to the farm stands and get some fresh corn. It was my custom over the years to make a crab and corn chowder on the first cool day at the end of summer. Rhonda and I had always called this the summer-is-ending dinner. This year there would be more people to invite, so I had to make a bigger pot. The chowder needed to sit over night to "ripen" the flavors.

"Ride!" I said to the sleeping Argus. Before I could grab my keys he was jumping at the door ready to go. We drove along route one until we came to a seafood truck that had pulled off to the side of the road to sell fish. I pulled up and bought a few pounds of fresh crab meat. I put the crab meat into an ice chest I brought along.

Next we drove out from route one through Dresden until we came to a farm stand. I bought some fresh ears of corn, some potatoes and onions. The farm stand also sold local milk and cream and butter, so I decided to stock up while I was there.

The ride back gave me some much-needed time to process the new developments. I was glad that Helga was alive and well. But I was sad that the victim was most likely someone else from my class. It was someone I should have known, but didn't. Had I been one of those cruel kids who shunned kids who weren't popular?

. . . .

I was putting the corn and crab chowder together when I saw Monica coming up the walkway. It must be my day for visitors.

209

"Come on in. I'm in the kitchen!" I yelled when she came to the door.

"It smells good. What are you making?"

"Corn and crab chowder. You want to come to dinner tomorrow?" I asked.

"Sure, can I…"

"Bring a friend?" I finished her sentence for her. "If that friend is Jason, sure!"

"He is such a sweet guy. Nothing like my soon-to-be ex!"

"That's good. Jason's always been a good friend."

"So what's up with you?" Monica asked.

"I'm working on my galley proofs for the cookbook and will be sending them back. I guess it's really going to be published."

"That's cool. But I sense that something else is going on with you," said Monica looking at me closely.

"How do you know that?" I asked.

"Grandma," she answered.

"Grandma? What does that mean? Have you been talking to the dead?" I asked, only half joking as I was cutting the corn off the cob to add to the chowder.

"No, I had a dream and in the dream Grandma told me that you needed my help."

"You know I'm not sure if I believe any of the spiritualist stuff we grew up with," I replied.

"Well, I'm not sure either, but it seems like when I follow my intuition, it usually works out."

"Okay, so what are you suppose to help me with?" I asked.

'Well, I'm not really sure," she answered. "Grandma didn't say."

"Well, Tim and I are working on the murder case. I found the body in my backyard and that is bothering me. Maybe another set of eyes will see something we keep missing." I took the pot of chowder and placed it in the refrigerator for tomorrow night.

"Sure, I'll do what I can."

"How about some coffee on the back porch, and I'll fill you in about what I know so far. Which isn't all that much."

Argus was sleeping in Monica's lap as I finished giving her the details as I knew them. I omitted the part about Helga being alive because Tim told me not to.

"So you think Jason being shot, your garage being set on fire, and your answer machine being hacked are somehow involved in a murder that took place thirty-five years ago?" Monica asked.

"Well, it sounds improbable when I say it out loud, but yes I do."

"No, not really. There is no statute of limitation on murder, and whoever did it is most likely still alive, and you've uncovered something that he or she thought was buried and forgotten. If they shot Jason, then they might shoot you. Be careful." Monica warned.

"There's something very wrong here, I can feel it," I said.

"Yes, I can feel it too. There something evil going on," Monica agreed.

Chapter 27

The cold air mass from Canada was still with us the next day; a reminder that fall was coming. It was early evening and it was already dark outside, another sign of the changing seasons. I knew summer would return, but this was a little taste of the future.

Everyone was gathered around my kitchen table with drinks in hand. Jason and Monica had gin and tonics, Rhonda and Jackson were drinking white wine, and Tim and I were drinking summer ale. I had just finished putting biscuits in the oven and sat down.

"Jesse and I have been doing this for the last twenty years. This is the first end-of-summer dinner that neither of us has had to go back to school," Rhonda said.

"To hell with back-to-school!" I toasted and everybody took a drink.

"Anybody else planning to retire?" asked Monica.

"Two more years," said Tim.

"Same here," answered Jason.

"I've already retired once!" said Jackson. I realized how little I know about him.

"What did you retire from?" I asked.

"I spent twenty-five years in the military before I went into insurance," said Jackson.

"Which agency do you work for?" Jason asked.

"Mid-Coast Associates," answered Jackson.

"Actually," said Rhonda beaming at him, "he owns the business."

I was taking the biscuits out of the oven while Jackson talked about his business. I put the biscuits in a basket on the table and began to ladle out chowder into bowls.

"I've never had corn and crab chowder, "said Tim. "It sure smells good."

"It takes the sting out of the end of summer," said Rhonda as she buttered her biscuit.

"Anything new on the Helga Johanson case?" asked Jackson.

"Yes, there is," said Tim. "I've sent the information to the state investigators, so I can talk about it now. The body is not Helga Johanson In fact Jesse and I met her a few days ago and she is very much alive!"

"But, I thought..." began Jason and then stopped. Tim filled everyone in on the recent developments, omitting the name of Brenda Wilson, since her identity hadn't been confirmed.

"So we don't know who it is then?" asked Jason.

"Not yet!" said Tim. "But we are working on it."

After we finished the meal we went into the living room and had chocolate cake and coffee. As happens in middle age, people began to excuse themselves as it got later. Tim stayed behind to help clean up.

"Thanks for not saying anything about Brenda Wilson," said Tim when we were alone.

"I took my cue from you. When you said the remains were unidentified, I knew not to say anything. Besides," I added, "we only have Helga's word for it. No proof."

"Well, in any case you've been a very good boy, and I've got something for you!"

"I'll bet you do!" I said.

. . . .

It was Sunday morning. The cold air mass had passed and summer returned with hot and humid air. The church doors were open to let in the breeze. Tim and I sat in the front. Monica and Jason sat with us, along with Jackson and Rhonda. All together we took up a whole pew. It was the last week in August and the church was full of tourists looking to soak up some New England spirituality.

I had come to respect Reverend Mary Bailey's gift for preaching. In fact I was beginning to lose my cynical view of organized religion. I had come to find All Souls as a community of diverse people who, if nothing else, were kind and caring of each other. To put it in words, I was beginning to feel at home.

After church I drove Rhonda and Jackson to Camden to begin their cruise on the *Doris Dean*. Argus was in heaven. Not only did he get a ride in the car, but also he had a choice of laps to sit in.

Parker Reed was on the ship to greet them and show them to their cabin. We all sat in the galley and had a beer before the other guests arrived. Parker and I took Argus for a walk around the harbor before he had to get back to his duties.

On the ride home I stopped at Red's Eats in Wiscasset. Argus and I sat in a chair while I ate my lobster roll and fries. I brought along some water and dog treats for Argus, so he could have a picnic, too.

The light was flashing on my new answer machine when I got home. The caller ID was no help as it said "unknown number" on it.

"Mind your own business," said the voice. It was a high falsetto voice in a stage whisper, which meant that it could either be a man or a woman.

I saved the message and called Tim.

"Join the club," he said when I told him about the message. "Jason called earlier and he got a message, too. Only his said 'next time I won't miss.'"

Chapter 28

Labor Day had come and gone, and I didn't have my annual panic attack at the thought of summer ending and nine months of hard work looming ahead. Today was the first day of school in Bath, and I wasn't the least bit sentimental about it. Despite the calendar saying that it was September, it was hard to find any evidence of it by the weather. It was still hot and humid, and I was glad not to be in a stuffy classroom on a nice day like this. Don't get me wrong; I loved teaching while I was doing it, and I would miss working with students, but it was time to move on.

Tim had offered to go and pick up Rhonda and Jackson as they disembarked from their cruise, so I was planning to go into work at Erebus and hear all about it. I made some yogurt muffins to take into work, and I was just taking them out of the oven when John Lowell came to the door. He had a copy of the *Times-Record* in his hand.

"Come in," I yelled from the kitchen.

"Good morning, Jesse, I thought you might like to see the paper this morning." He held up the paper for me to see the headlines. "BACKYARD REMAINS NOT THAT OF EXCHANGE STUDENT" read the main headlines. "MYSTERY REMAINS" read the tag line underneath. I quickly read the story.

"Thanks, John, for bringing this to me. Tim and I met with Helga in person. It was kind of spooky since all this time we thought she was dead." The paper made no mention of Brenda Wilson, since an identity had yet to be confirmed.

John and I chatted over coffee for a few minutes and then I harnessed up Argus, and we headed off to Erebus.

"Hey, sailor!" I said as I walked in the shop.

"Hey, yourself! Hi Argus!" said Rhonda has she bent down to pat Argus. When you have a pug, you get used to people greeting the dog with more enthusiasm than they use greeting you. "Who's a good boy?" The dog wagged his tail. Argus, of course thought the world revolved around him, which of course it does.

"How was the trip?" I asked.

"Oh, my God! It was the best trip ever! We sailed along the coast with only the sound of the wind in the sails. No electronics, no cell phones, no radio or TV. And the food! Oh my god, the food was so great!"

"I told you the fresh sea air would give you an appetite."

"We had the best time. The lobster bake on the island was the best! And the muffins first thing in the morning were to die for!"

"Like these?" I asked as I handed her the bag of yogurt muffins. "I got the recipe when I worked on the *Doris Dean*."

Rhonda took a bit. "These are great. Cooking on the ship with only a wood stove must be hard. How did you do it?"

"Well, it was fun," I said. "I only had to do it for a few weeks, and the passengers raved about the food, which is always good to hear. How were the other people?"

"There were twelve of us all together, and most of them were retired, so we all had something

217

in common. In fact we all booked a trip at the same time for next year."

"I knew you would enjoy it. And did Jackson like it?"

"The man can't sit still. He was into everything and ended up working as one of the crew. He hoisted the sail, helped pull up the anchor, and even took the wheel!"

"That's great! Brad and I held the fort here. He's gone back to school, but he'll be working from three to five in the afternoons whenever you need him." I told her.

"So," Rhonda said with a look on her face that I knew so well. "You and Parker Reed were an item?"

"We had some laughs," I said. "We shared the crew quarters when I was on board as the cook."

"Ah huh," said Rhonda. "I've heard that before."

"He and I have been friends for a long time."

"Yes, and now I know why you loved to go on those cruises."

I thought it was time to change the subject so I told her about the threats that Jason and I got on the phone.

"What is going on?" she asked. "Nothing seems to make sense."

"I think the answer is right in front of us, but we can't see it. I just have a feeling that I'm overlooking something."

The phone rang and Rhonda went to answer it. I waited on two customers who came into the shop. More customers entered as a fall tour bus stopped in town for a shopping break before setting of up the coast.

"That was Jane Foley from the church's board of deacons," said Rhonda when we had a chance to talk after the tourist left. "She was looking for volunteers for the Thanksgiving Outreach Committee. I told her we would both be happy to do it."

"You what?" I asked.

"You'll be great. We needed someone with food skills."

"You know I don't like committees," I said. "I just can't keep my mouth shut when I'm on a committee."

"I know. It's kind of fun to watch you!"

"Well, this time I'm going to keep my mouth shut and keep my opinions to myself," I said.

"Sure," said Rhonda. "That'll happen!" And then she laughed.

. . . .

Tim walked over from the police station and picked me up for lunch. We walked down to the waterfront to Ruby's. We sat outside because it was such a nice day and there was no wind. I ordered a beer, and Tim had ice tea since he had to go back to work.

"We are out straight this time of year," said Tim. "I have to have extra officers on duty when school starts up again."

"Back in Manchester we had to have police officers in the schools."

"Well, at least we don't have to do that yet. In fact we don't get called to the schools very often."

219

"I've always wondered what it would be like to teach at Morse High."

"You could be a substitute teacher," offered Tim.

"Yes," I answered. "And pigs could fly out of my butt! Do you know what my students used to call the subs?"

"No, what?"

"Open season!"

Our sandwiches arrived and we ate in silence for a few minutes. Then Tim grew serious.

"We have to figure out what's going on. I don't like people leaving threats on your machine and I don't like people shooting at Jason."

"I've been thinking about this," I said. "Somehow Jason is the key to this whole thing. I just can't figure out how."

"I think you're right. Somehow Jason is more of a threat to someone than you are."

"Do you think that these last two calls were made by Rita Toliver? Whoever she is."

"It could be. It might be the same phone, or it could be a new one. It's impossible to trace prepaid cell phones."

"What happened when you guys tried to call the cell phone?" I asked.

"Nothing, it just went to an automated voice message. Either the phone wasn't on or she wasn't answering it."

"When you go back to the office, will you look up the number and give it to me?" I asked.

Tim proceeded to rattle off the number. "You remember the number?" I asked.

"Yes, it's a cop thing."

I opened my cell phone and began pressing keys.

"What are you doing? Tim asked me.

"I'm sending a text message to the number. He or she isn't going to answer the phone, but she might be curious enough to read a text message. If she or he does, someone will get a surprise. And if this turns out to be nothing, no harm done.

"What did you say in the message? " Tim asked when I finished sending it.

"I said, 'I know who you are and what you've done' and I signed it 'J. A.'"

"The problem with this is that you don't know who you are dealing with, and you don't know what they've done, or even if this has anything to do with anything."

"Well, if it is connected, this may help to flush out whoever is behind this," I said.

"And get yourself in danger!" said Tim.

"I taught high school kids," I said. "Nothing can scare me!"

Chapter 29

Jane Foley addressed the committee, "This year, in addition to our usual Thanksgiving baskets for those who have fallen on hard times, I thought we should host Thanksgiving dinner at our church for the homeless."

"What a great idea," said Rhonda. The others in room nodded their heads in agreement. There were six of us on the committee. As often happens in my life, I was the only guy on the committee.

"I can let some of my clients know about it. It would be great for them," offered Barbara Sewell. She was a social worker who worked in the small downtown office for a non-profit social justice agency.

I was determined for once to be quiet and wait until I was asked.

"We could have the dinner earlier in the day and that would leave us time to get back to our families," said Betty Loomis. I was pretty sure Betty Loomis wouldn't know a poor person if she stepped over one.

"I think that might appear to be condescending," I said. So much for my vow of silence! I looked at Rhonda and saw her suppressing laughter. "We have lots of single people and empty-nesters in church, not to mention the elderly. Why don't we have a Thanksgiving dinner for our church members and then invite others to join us? That way we are sharing what we have, rather than giving what we can spare."

"Jesse," said the Reverend Mary Bailey, "that's perfect! It's the Christian thing to do." We all looked at Barbara Sewell. "What do you think, Barbara? You know better than anyone."

"I think there is a huge difference between a handout and an invitation," said Barbara.

"It will also be great for some of the older women in our church. They can make some of their favorite dishes and bring them to share. Many of them love to cook, but have no one to cook for," said Mary Bailey.

"And Jesse," said Rhonda, "would be happy to cook the turkeys." I shot her my killer look.

"Our kitchen," continued Mary Bailey "is a huge, professional-style kitchen that would rival most restaurants." This was true. I had snooped around in there once and was impressed with the set up.

"And I know Rhonda would love to coordinate all the menu items and donations of food for the dinner," I said as I shot her my most evil smile.

"Great!" said Jane Foley. "We are lucky to have you two with us."

After the meeting when we were outside Rhonda turned to be and said, "Asshole! Putting me in charge!"

"That's for offering my services as chef, bitch!" I said sweetly.

"What are friends for?" We both laughed.

Tim was waiting for me on the front porch when I got home. I could tell by his face that something was up. We went into the house, and I let Argus out of his crate. Tim made a fuss over Argus while I opened two beers and we headed to the back porch. After the first sip he began.

"The state investigators called me with a positive ID. They were able to get Brenda Wilson's medical records. She had several broken bones when she was in school and they were able to find evidence on the bones that was consistent with healed fractures. I would say by the number of fractures that she was also an abused child. It's all a little disturbing."

"Wow! Is this public knowledge?" I asked.

"It will be in a day or two. The medical examiner will give a statement to the press."

"Do you think Bitch Blair had anything to do with it?" I asked.

"Helga seemed to think so. And I think that's enough for me to bring her in for questioning," said Tim between sips of beer.

"I want to be there!" I said with some venom.

"Now we also have to figure out what Jason Goulet has to do with this all. We haven't yet looked at this from the Brenda Wilson angle."

"I'll invite him over for a guys' night. The Red Sox have a game on Saturday. Are you free or do you have to work?" I asked.

"I'm free for the whole weekend," replied Tim.

"When are you going to question Bitch Blair?"

"I'll have to coordinate with the Portland police. I'll let you know."

. . . .

Maine has a short growing season and the harvest time was here. I made the rounds of the local farm stands and bought as much fresh produce as I could. I'm a great advocate of buying locally available produce, and this year I had the time to can and freeze vegetables. Freezing was easy, but canning takes preparation. Today I was canning tomatoes in jars. Since tomatoes are acidy, I was able to use the simpler water bath for canning.

On the stove I had a big pot of stewed tomatoes, and I was busy spooning the tomatoes into jars and placing the jars in boiling water. I was looking forward to hot soups on cold days. Just as I finished up a batch the phone rang.

"Hi, Jesse!" It was Janice Shepard-Swanson, my literary agent and, of course, Rhonda's sister.

"Hi, Janice. What's up?"

"I just talked to the publisher and your book is finished and you should get a copy of it today or tomorrow. I'm excited."

"Wow, I guess it's really going to happen. I can't wait."

"I've got a copy here on my desk and it looks great!"

After she hung up I called my parents in Florida, then Rhonda and Monica. I'd tell Tim when he stopped by later. It was hard to go back to canning with any excitement now. I couldn't wait for the mail to come.

Argus and I were sitting on the front porch waiting for the mailman. Rhonda and Monica had both come over to wait with me and see the cookbook. The mailman was usually as punctual as the sun, but of course today he was half an hour late.

When he finally pulled onto the street it seemed to take an eternity for him to deliver the mail to the neighbors. When he finally handed me the package, I turned it over and over in my hands afraid to open it.

"Open the fucking thing!" said Rhonda. "Monica and I have been sitting here for an hour."

"Here goes!" I said as I slit the top on the package and turned out the cookbook. I stared at the cookbook in horror!

The photo of me in cut-off jeans and plastic flip-flops wasn't just a small photo on the back dust jacket. It was the dust jacket! There I was sitting on the steps of a trailer with the title White Trash Cooking! centered over my head.

Monica and Rhonda were laughing so hard I thought they would pee their pants!

It got worse as I flipped through the pages. Interspersed throughout the book were full-page photos of me cooking in the trailer's kitchen? And they were in color!

Now, don't get me wrong. I'm not a snob. It's just that I take great pride in the way I dress. I've never worn a white tee shirt or cut-off jeans. And I would never, ever wear flip-flops on my feet. In fact I have quite a few pairs of shoes. One time my students kept track of my shoes and were astounded when for a whole month I wore different shoes every day.

"It's not funny!" I said.

"The hell it's not!" said Rhonda roaring with laughter.

"Jesse," said Monica doubled over and gasping for breath, "This is even better than my final divorce decree!"

Chapter 30

I was sitting in the police cruiser next to Tim. We were going to Portland to question Judy Blair. And by "we" I mean Tim. Tim had hoped to catch her by surprise. The identification of Brenda Wilson had not yet been made public, so Judy wouldn't know about the new developments.

Tim was going to question Judy at the Portland Police station. I had no official standing in the investigation, but I was going to view the questioning from behind a one-way mirror. Tim had arranged for my presence by calling in a few favors.

"I had them keep Bitch Blair overnight in the jail cell, just to shake her up a bit," said Tim. He was wearing his cop face today, so I couldn't read his emotions.

"Can you do that?" I asked.

"Sure, but we have a time limit. After that we have to charge her or let her go free. Unless we can shake a confession out of her, we will never be able to charge her on Helga's suspicion.

"Maybe Helga just wanted to give Judy Blair a bad day." I observed.

"Maybe, if so she succeeded."

The interrogation room at the Portland Police Department looked just like a movie set. There were several metal chairs and a metal table. There was a strong overhead light and that was about it. I sat in the next room watching through the one-way mirror. I had a cup of coffee and a donut, and a much more comfortable chair. It was like watching TV.

Tim was teamed up with a Portland detective named Bryan Day. When a female police officer brought Judy Blair into the room, I was almost sorry for her. Almost, but not quite. Judy looked ghastly when she was brought in. No make-up and not very much sleep. That's one of the problems with being middle age. We can fix ourselves up, but illness or lack of sleep shows up in our faces, no matter what we do.

As the questioning began I could tell right away that Tim and Bryan were playing good cop / bad cop. Bryan was the bad cop and Tim, because he knew the suspect, was the good cop. It must take a certain amount of acting skill to be a cop. Both of them were playing their roles well. I was glad I wasn't the suspect.

Another detective named Winston Grant joined me in the observation room.

"What do you think so far?" he asked.

"She seems rattled, but that's to be expected I should think."

"You'd be surprised by how cool some of the suspects are," he said.

"Can you tell if a suspect is lying?" I asked.

"Usually, but it's not an exact science."

We watched Judy's expression as Tim told her that the body was not that of Helga, but was Brenda Wilson. I thought that her expression was one of shock rather than just surprise. Then Judy asked who Brenda was and claimed she didn't know anybody by that name.

"She's lying," said Winston.

"I agree. And she's not a good liar either."

Tim left the room and Bryan began his bad cop routine in earnest. It was uncomfortable to watch. Judy was crying and Bryan was trying to break her down. Finally Bryan walked out.

Tim and Bryan came into the observation room.

"Are you guys done?" I asked.

"No," said Tim. "We're just letting her sit there by herself for a while, and then I'll go back in and play the old high school chum."

"What do you think Winston?" asked Bryan.

"She's lying about knowing the deceased."

"I think so, too," said Tim.

"Time for act two," said Tim and he slipped into the interrogation room.

The questioning went on for two more hours but it was becoming clear that Judy Blair wasn't going to confess, or for that matter give any new information.

"That's tough work!" I said to Tim on the drive home.

"It's not fun. But you have to look at the bigger picture. We are looking for a killer. If I make a few people uncomfortable along the way, that's too bad. Brenda Wilson's killer deserves to be found."

"She lying about knowing Brenda," I said.

"I know, but lying isn't an admission of murder. It's not even a crime really."

"What next?" I asked.

"If we can link Judy Blair to Rita Toliver, or better yet prove that she is Rita Toliver, we might get her. And tomorrow we'll talk to Jason and try to find out why he's being targeted."

Stephen E. Stanley

. . . .

The Red Sox had won two World Series in the past few years. Everyone in New England remembers where he or she was when the 'curse was reversed' in 2004 and the sox won the series for the first time since 1918! In 2007 the Sox won again. This year they were having a good season, so there was always hope of another win. Today the Sox were playing their great rivals the Yankees.

I was in the kitchen setting up the snack food for the game. I had prepared buffalo chicken wings, cheese and crackers, chip and dip, and I also made a pizza to pop in the oven later.

"How many people are you feeding?" asked Tim when he came into the kitchen looking for me.

"You think it's too much?" I asked.

"Not if you're inviting the entire police department!"

"Always better to have too much than too little. Besides, Jason is a big guy, and I've seen you eat a few times too."

Tim checked the beer supply in the refrigerator. "I think we're pretty well prepared."

"Unless the game goes into overtime."

"Well, we have a few hours before the game starts and Jason should be here anytime now. The medical examiner will release the details tomorrow and then it will be in all the papers," Tim said.

"Anyone home?" yelled Jason through the screen door before he walked in.

"Beer?" I asked.

"Absolutely," he replied.

I took the plate of cheese and crackers and we headed out to the back porch. Argus trailed behind us and took up his position in the middle of the room. Pugs like to be in the middle of the action, even when there isn't any actual action.

"Anymore threats?" I asked Jason.

"No, you?" he asked.

"No," I answered.

"Jesse," asked Tim, "Did you ever get a reply from the text message you sent to the mystery phone?"

"Actually Tim, I haven't even turned on my cell phone in days. It's somewhere in my car."

"Jesse sent an email to the prepaid cell phone that was registered to Rita Toliver. It's the one that the threats come in on. We haven't been able to trace it." Tim said to fill Jason in on the development."

"What did you write?" asked Jason.

"I know who you are and what you've done, or something like that," I told him.

"Jason," Tim went into cop mode. "Do you have any idea why you are being targeted?"

"No, I've thought about it a lot. I really can't think of any link with the death."

"Jason," said Tim, "Do you remember Brenda Wilson from high school?"

Jason thought for a moment. "Yes, I do. She was very quiet and was picked on a lot, I think."

"The medical examiner has identified the remains as Brenda Wilson."

Jason turned pale and was shaking so hard he had to put his glass of beer down.

"Jason, what's the matter?" I asked.

"I might have seen her get killed!"

Chapter 31

The summer had been warm and dry, with only a few showers here and there. Now it was September and rain was needed. Everything in the garden that wasn't watered on a regular basis was drying up. The drought was turning the leaves earlier than usual. The swamp maples had already turned red, an indication of the coming autumn colors.

Dark storm clouds were gathering in the sky threatening a much needed rain. If it rained too hard, the rain would knock out my satellite reception and Jason, Tim, and I would end up listening to the Red Sox game on the radio.

"What do you mean you think you saw her get killed?" Tim asked as Jason twisted uncomfortably in his chair.

"It was sometime after we graduated. There was a party here at Eagle's Nest. I was smoking pot with Judy Blair. Brenda Wilson was here. I knew her from history class. She was very quiet, but she came here to party a few times. Bitch Blair always picked on her. I had wandered off to see who else might be around when I heard a commotion. I went to look and I saw Brenda Wilson screaming at someone at the top of her lungs. She and the other person were physically fighting. The other person picked up a fallen tree limb and hit her with it. I thought the fight was so loud that the police would be showing up. I ran to my car and drove home. I didn't want to be found by the police when I was stoned. I expected to read about the fight and the party in the newspaper, but I didn't see anything, so I thought that it probably wasn't anything. I didn't know that she had been killed."

"Who was the other person?" I asked.

"That's just it. I didn't get a close look. It was dark, and I was too far away to see. I didn't hear a voice other than Brenda's."

"But apparently, the killer thinks that you saw him or her and doesn't know that you didn't really see who it was," observed Tim.

"Was anybody else there?" I asked.

"There were probably twenty or so people, but most were inside. I didn't see anyone else in the back, but they must have heard it," Jason was looking pale as the truth was setting in.

"What does all this mean?" I asked Tim.

Tim took a deep breath. "Up to now the killer hasn't been too concerned because we misidentified the body. The threats against you and Jason have just been insurance so we wouldn't look too closely. Tomorrow when the medical examiner releases the true identity, you both will be in danger. "Jason, if you saw the murder, then the killer will be after you. And you, Ashes," said Tim using his nickname for me, "you could be in danger because you've been asking too many questions."

"Jason," I asked, "do you remember when this took place?"

"I only went one time after graduation. New people moved into the house at the end of June. I worked at the hospital that summer and I only had Mondays off, so it must have been Sunday night."

"We can look up the date and that will give us an estimate of the time of death," said Tim.

"Where was Bitch Blair during all this?" I asked. "You said she was there with you."

"She wandered off sometime during the evening. I thought she must have gone home. I lost track of her. What do we do now?" asked Jason.

I looked at my watch. "I suggest we think about it a little bit more and in the mean time we watch the Red Sox bury the Yankees!"

The rain did come and it rained hard all night. I did lose the satellite signal during the rain, and we did end up listening to the game on the radio. The Sox didn't bury the Yankees, but the score was tied at one point and it was very exciting until the end of the game. With all the food I made and with the excitement of the game, we were able to forget about threats and murders for a few hours.

The next morning the rain and stopped and the air was much colder than it had been. I harnessed up Argus for his morning walk when John Lowell flagged me down as I walked by his house. He held up the *Times-Record's* front page. "MYSTERY SOLVED; REMAINS INDENTIFIED" read the headlines. Dorothy came out onto their front porch.

"I had Brenda Wilson in third grade," she said. "Such a quiet girl, she was."

"Was she in my class?" I asked. I didn't remember her and I had Mrs. Lowell as my third grade teacher.

"No, I don't think so. I think she stayed back in second grade. I remember her parents died and she missed a lot of school."

"How do you remember all this?" I asked her. I was lucky if I could remember where I put my reading glasses down.

"It was my first year teaching. She was one of my first students. That's why I could remember. Don't you remember your first students?" she asked.

"Oh, yes. I remember them. I couldn't tell you the names of any of my students in the last five years, but the first year I remember very clearly."

We chatted some more and then Argus and I continued on our way. I was going to work all day at Erebus, so I thought I would put something in the crock-pot for dinner when I got home later.

I cut up some Italian sausages, opened a frozen package of lima beans, threw in a can of kidney beans, and another can of cannelloni beans in the pot. I cut up and onion and a green pepper, and opened a can of tomato sauce, threw them in the pot, and put the cover on. It would simmer all day and be ready when I got home.

I put Argus in the car and we drove to work. I didn't want to walk and end up walking home in the rain, though I was sure Rhonda would take us home if need be.

I remembered my cell phone and opened my glove compartment and turned it on. I was planning to call Tim before I went into work. As soon as the phone booted up it made a chirping sound that was different then my usual ring tone. I looked at the small screen and it said "1 new message." I hit the select button and read the message. It said "Bye Bye RT." Someone had read and responded to my text message!

I saved the message and called Tim. He wasn't in his office so I left a message and went in to work.

Erebus had come a long way during the year and a half that Rhonda had opened the shop. At first she carried the typical gift shop items that one can find in any coastal gift shop. There just wasn't a market for ceramic lighthouses and plastic lobster claws. Gradually Rhonda added crafts from local artisans along with some upscale objects d'art. All of these were also offered on her website. In addition, both the shop and the website carried various occult paraphernalia.

It was my job to keep the website updated and fill the Internet orders. What had started as a part-time job for a few hours a week was beginning to expand into several days a week.

When I walked through the door Rhonda quickly looked up to see if I had brought any baked goods with me. Not that it really mattered; one of us would walk down the street later and buy some pastries.

"Guess what's in the box?" Rhonda asked by way a greeting.

"George Bush voodoo dolls?" I asked.

"Nope, but that's an excellent idea. I bet we could sell tons of them."

"Okay," I said. "What's in the box?"

"Cookbooks!" She opened the box and I saw my picture splashed on the cover of about two dozen cookbooks.

"You think you'll sell that many?" I asked.

"Oh, yes. Just look at the cover!"

"Very funny!"

"Would you sign them? Then I can sell them as autographed copies."

I sighed. I was going to take a lot of ribbing for this, I was sure.

At two in the afternoon I was still sitting at my computer when Tim walked into the back room of the shop. Argus jumped up from his nap and ran to greet him.

"I just got your message. What's up?"

"Take a look at this." I showed him the saved message on my cell phone.

"Damn, I've about had it with all this shit. I better call Jason and see if he's gotten any warnings."

"Tim, I just have a feeling that we're missing something. Like we have all the pieces but we can't figure out the design."

"Sooner or later someone is going to give himself or herself away. I'm still betting on Bitch Blair."

"Wishful thinking! You just want to see her get the chair."

"We don't have capital punishment here, remember?"

"I was speaking metaphorically," I said.

"Metaphor this!" said Tim with a wink and then was gone.

. . . .

I drove home, and just as I suspected the rain had returned. I fed Argus and then dished out a plate of three-bean casserole for myself. I picked the high school yearbook off the shelf and started to look through it. It still bothered me that I couldn't remember Brenda Wilson.

I was randomly flipping through the pages when I saw another picture of her. She was in the drama club technical crew photo. There were three kids posed around two spotlights. One of the kids was Brenda Wilson. The second kid was Ben Jacobs, who was a junior that year, but the third person was someone I didn't expect to see. In fact he said he didn't remember Brenda Wilson at all, but there in the picture was a very young Tim Mallory!

Chapter 32

It was the third meeting of the church's Thanksgiving committee. "We've had several generous donations for the Thanksgiving outreach dinner. Several local merchants have stepped forward. Rhonda Shepard has donated centerpieces for the tables," said Deacon Jane Foley. I thought donating the centerpieces was a very clever way for Rhonda to get rid of some ceramic lighthouses we had in the back room.

"I think we should put an invitation in the newspaper for anyone to come who wants to," I said.

"That's a great idea, Jesse," replied Reverend Mary Bailey.

"We could have a free will offering to help defray expenses," offered Betty Loomis. "You know this is going to cost us money!"

"How kind of you to offer!" said Rhonda with just an edge of sarcasm that I knew would be lost on Betty. "How much can we expect from you?" Betty sputtered something that we couldn't hear and looked embarrassed.

"This is Thanksgiving," I said. "We are not taking money from anyone! If someone wants to bring a favorite dish to the meal, we'll take it. But I don't think we need to embarrass our guests."

"I agree," said Jane Foley. "No collection!"

"Rhonda," asked Mary Bailey. "You're organizing everything. Are we ready?"

"We've got donations of turkeys from Bryson's Market. People in the congregation have offered to bring in side dishes and pies. Jesse is in charge of the kitchen. We have a full staff available to help cook, serve, and clean up. Yes, we are ready."

"Will we have enough food?" asked Barbara Sewell.

"How many invitations have you given out to your clients?" I asked.

"Around fifty, but I've also told them to invite anyone else they can think of."

"We should have more than enough food. Everyone has been very generous." I said. "If we have any leftovers, we can send them home with people."

"I hope we are going to use paper plates if you are going to have all those people in here," grumbled Betty Loomis.

I thought for a moment that Rhonda was going to slap her for the "those people" comment. I certainly would have loved to see Betty's pearls hit the floor.

"We'll use our best china to make our guests feel at home," Mary Bailey said sweetly to Betty.

"Betty Loomis needs her clock cleaned!" whispered Rhonda to me.

"Oh, yes," I whispered back.

Indian summer in Maine is by far its best season. It is warm during the days and cool at night. The autumn colors are brilliant and the roads are crowded with leaf peepers who have driven north to see the fall spectacle. The only down side to this season was the shortening of the days. Most of the flowers were gone, and we all knew that winter would come.

Some years the autumn rains come just as the leaves turn and by the time the sun returns the leaves has been beaten off the trees. This year there was no rain in sight and the tourists were flocking to Maine.

Erebus had seen an increase in business as the tour buses pulled up on Front Street every morning.

Monica Ashworth-Twist sat in a rocking chair on my front porch sipping on a glass of Moxie.

"I want," said Monica between sips, "to get whoever shot Jason!"

"You're in love, aren't you?" It wasn't really a question.

"Yes, I am. Jason is kind and smart, and he doesn't have a mean bone in his body. I don't want anything to happen to him," she said. "Or to you either, Jesse!" she added as an afterthought.

"The trouble is," I said, "I know I'm missing something. The fact that both Jason and I have been threatened means that the killer is still around. It also means that the killer thinks that we know more than we do."

"You remember what our grandmother taught us?" she asked.

"Listen to your inner voice," I said.

"And your inner voice is telling you that all the clues are there and that you need to fit the clues together."

"Yes," I agreed.

"Well then, we are going to piece this together."

"The problem is I'm not sure I really want to know. I have a feeling I know the killer. It could be anyone."

"What are you really afraid of," Monica asked.

"Tim lied about knowing Brenda Wilson!" I said and then had to look away.

"How do you know?" she asked.

"I saw a picture of them together in the high school yearbook. They were both lighting techs for the drama club. Yet Tim said he didn't remember her."

"Well, maybe he really doesn't remember her. Do you remember everyone from high school?"

"No, I guess not," I said, but I wasn't convinced.

"Okay then, let's eliminate some people for a start."

"I know I didn't do it. You didn't do it, and Rhonda didn't do it."

"That's a start." She said.

"Let's go for a walk." I wanted to change the subject.

"Show me around the house and tell me what you've done to the place."

We walked around the house and I showed her the gardens I had put in. "I had the house insulated, new windows put in, a new roof, and the whole place painted yellow."

"I love what you've done."

"This was all weeds and brush," I said as I waved my hand at back yard.

"There's bad energy here!" said Monica. She was standing in the middle of a patch of faded wild flowers.

"Right where you're standing is where I dug up the remains. I was trying to dig a place for vegetables."

Monica shivered. "Show me where the fire was."

We walked over to the garage. I opened the overhead door to let in light. "The fire was over in that corner."

"You still have packing boxes stored here," she observed.

"Along with my car, the snow blower, and my bicycle." I said as I looked around. And then as I looked at my bicycle, something clicked in.

"That's it!" I yelled. "That's the missing piece. The bicycle is the answer. I know who shot Jason and probably killed Brenda Wilson!"

It was getting dark as Monica and I sat down for supper. I had made some baked beans earlier in the week and we were having bean sandwiches. I had put a spoonful of beans on toast, placed bacon and cheese on top, and had broiled them in the oven.

"Are you going to tell Tim," Monica asked.

"Not yet. I'm not sure what to tell him. I can't tell him I know who the killer is, and the only evidence I have is my gut feeling to do on."

"So how are you going to prove who the killer is?"

"I'm going to shake the tree until something falls out."

"Be careful," said Monica.

"I think Jason is in more danger than I am. I know this is going to be a hardship for you, but I want you to move in with Jason."

"Some hardship!" she said with a laugh.

"I'm serious. I want you to drive him to work and pick him up at night and never let him out of your sight. If you are around it will discourage anyone from trying anything."

"What about you?" Monica asked with concern.

"Tim has an irregular schedule. He shows up at odd times and sometimes stays here if he's free. Having a cop popping in and out is a good deterrent."

After dinner when Monica had left for Jason's I called Judy Blair. I thought this was a good place to start shaking the tree.

"Hi, Judy. It's Jesse. How are you?"

"Just great, what do you want, Jesse?"

"Well, I just wanted to give you some good news. I figured out who killed Brenda Wilson, so you are off the hook."

There was a pause on the other end. "Who did it?" she asked.

"I really don't want to say yet. I'm planning to take the evidence to the police on Monday, once I've gathered everything together."

"Good for you," she said and hung up. I wasn't at all sure that she wasn't somehow involved. I figured if nothing else she would be on the phone and telling everybody she knew that I was going to reveal the killer. It couldn't hurt.

Chapter 33

The days were getting noticeably shorter on both ends. It was dark when I got up in the morning. Argus didn't care if it was dark or not as long as he got out to relieve himself and got a bowl of dog food.

I missed the morning sunshine, but now I was able to see the sunrise as I had my morning coffee. The house was chilly, and I finally had to break down and turn the furnace on. I knew that once I did it, that the heat would be on until April.

I sat with my toast and coffee and tried to figure out what to do next. I wanted to give that tree another shake because I thought I was close to the truth. Still there was always the chance that I was wrong.

When I knew that Becky and Bill Simpson were most likely at work I called their answer machine and left a message. "Hi Bill, it's Jesse. Give me a call. It's urgent that I talk to you."

My next call was to Tim. I knew he wasn't working today so I called his house. He either wasn't home or he wasn't answering the phone, so I left a similar message for him. Now all I had to do was wait.

The housekeeping fairies had failed to appear again, so I ended up on vacuum cleaner duty. I had neglected dust and clutter for the last several days in favor of working outside, but now I had to attend to cleaning and fixing up the inside of the house. Since I was waiting around anyway, I figured I might as well be busy.

By the time the house was spotless I was beginning to think that I had been mistaken. My phone calls hadn't stirred anyone up. Neither Tim nor Bill had returned my phone calls, and I was aware that I might have to think up something new.

It was dark outside. The sun had set and there was no moon and very little light from anywhere. For some reason I have excellent night vision so I took Argus outside for a little walk. Argus and I were off in the side yard when I saw some movement up the street out of the corner of my eye.

I took Argus to the backyard and tied his leash around a fence pole. I didn't want him in the way if I had to confront someone. I stepped behind a holly bush in the front yard as the figure got closer.

"Nice evening!" I said as I stepped out from behind the bush.

The figure jumped back. "Oh Jesse, you startled me!" said Becky Simpson.

"What are you doing here Becky?" I asked.

"I'm, ah, looking for Bill. You left a message on the answer machine for him, and I thought he might be here."

"I'll bet Bill didn't get the message. I'll bet you got home first, played the message and then erased it. I'll bet you're pretty good with answer machines."

"I don't know what you're talking about."

"Nice try Becky! Shall I fill in the blanks for you?"

"You don't know what you are talking about," she said with a hysterical tone to her voice.

247

"The only thing I don't understand is how you knew where Dr. Jacobs' dental records were stored."

"I worked in his office until he retired. I guess you're not as good as you think you are." Becky had an expression of rage on her face at this point. "Not that the information is going to do you any good." Becky took a step close to me.

"You're right Becky, I missed that one. But you left some other clues around." I continued. "It was the bicycle. Bill and I were talking and he mentioned that you bike. Someone on a bike was seen around the time Jason was shot and around the time when a warning was placed on my car. That was the giveaway."

"You can't prove anything!"

"And then when you sent that text message and signed it RT. You thought I would think it stood for Rita Toliver. But RT made me think of your maiden name, Rebecka Todd!"

"Well, you aren't going to get the chance to tell anyone." Becky reached into her pocket and brought out a gun. "And Jason won't be telling anyone either."

"Hey, Becky, do you think I'm stupid? I've already told people. And what you don't know is that Jason didn't even see the person who killed Brenda Wilson. So you see Becky, all of this was for nothing. So tell me why you killed her?"

"Brenda deserved to die. She was a bitch when she got stoned. She was taunting me, telling me that Bill didn't really love me. She said he really liked to fool around. She said some mean things. I didn't mean to kill her but; I wanted to shut her up."

"So who helped you to bury her? I'm sure you couldn't do that alone."

"Judy Blair helped me to bury her. She swore that she would never tell." Becky was waving the gun as she talked. "Now I want you to walk quietly to the car."

"I don't think so," I said as I refused to move. She jammed the gun in my ribs. Suddenly the air was filled with an ear-piercing wail. Argus didn't like being left alone in the back yard and was making it known. Becky was startled at the sound. I reached behind me and grabbed the hoe that I had left leaning on the bush when I was doing yard work. I smacked Becky in the arm with it, and the gun went flying. She yelled out in pain and dove in the direction of the gun.

As she reached for the gun again I brought the hoe down on her hand and heard a sickening crunch just as she screamed out in pain.

Becky sat there sobbing and rocking her smashed hand. "You can't prove anything!" She sobbed.

I reached into my pocket and pulled out a small digital recorder. "You want to bet?" I asked. Off in the distance I heard Tim Mallory's truck rumbling down the street.

. . . .

Monica had stopped at Wong Ho's and picked up Chinese food for dinner. Tim, Rhonda, Jason and I sat around my kitchen table.

"Why didn't you let me know what you were doing?" asked Tim.

"I had no proof. If I brought you in and I was wrong, your job would be on the line. She could claim police harassment or something." I said.

"Weren't you afraid?" asked Jason.

"Ever stare down a room full of hostile teenagers? I also borrowed one of Tim's Kevlar vests, so I had some protection. I felt a little foolish wearing it because I wasn't sure she would show up, but she did."

"What's going to happen now?" Rhonda asked Tim.

"The Portland police picked up Judy Blair. She will be tried as an accessory to man slaughter. If she works out a deal and testifies against Becky, she gets a lighter sentence. Becky Simpson, on the other hand, isn't going to see daylight for a long, long time."

The food was disappearing quickly as we all loaded up our plates for the second time. I noticed that Jason and Monica were holding hands and seemed cozy.

'I hope it wasn't too uncomfortable for you," I said to Jason, "to have Monica move in with you."

"It was a sacrifice," replied Jason with a mock sigh, "but we got through it, okay"

"In fact," said Monica, "I have no intention of moving out. Just in case Becky escapes from jail, you understand."

"And you," Tim turned to me, "Let me do the police work next time."

"Sure thing chief! In fact, I think someone may have broken into my bedroom. Maybe you could check it out later?" I said.

"Anything for a citizen," said Tim with a smile.

. . . .

"In the midst of life we are in death, from whom can we seek help?" The Reverend Mary Bailey read from the Psalms over the grave of Brenda Wilson.

A large group had gathered as we interred the ashes near a large memorial stone in Oak Grove Cemetery. Brenda had no family or friends, and since she was found in my backyard I was allowed to take charge of the arrangements.

I had intended to quietly and anonymously buy a small marker and grave, but word got out and many of my former classmates collected money and we were able to provide Brenda with a proper burial. It was a time of sadness and reflection, but I think each of us vowed to treat others better. It was a lesson we learned too late for Brenda Wilson, but maybe, just maybe, we could do better next time.

At the final prayer we held hands in a circle around the grave. The sun that had been hiding all morning behind a dark cloud, broke free from the gloom and rain and shined brightly on the planet as we departed in silence.

Chapter 34

November was one of my favorite months. It was clear and cold, but the snow had yet to come. There seemed to be more light as the trees had shed their leaves. The sea and sky were a brilliant shade of dark blue and the green of the evergreens softened the harsh brown and gold of late autumn.

There were over eighty people gathered this Thanksgiving in the parish hall of All Souls Church. It was more than we planned for, but we also had much more food than we knew what to do with. There would be enough food for seconds and thirds, and still some left for people to take home.

I gave the signal that all the food was ready.

"Attention everyone," yelled Reverend Mary Bailey. "I've been told that the food is about ready. I want to give a special welcome to our guests for joining us. Your presence does us a great honor. I also want to thank the Thanksgiving outreach committee for arranging this great community celebration. Special thanks go out to Rhonda Shepard, who organized this day, and to Jesse Ashworth, our chief cook." Everyone clapped at this point.

"Before we say grace and dig into this great buffet I want to share two joys with you. The first is that Rhonda Shepard and Jesse Ashworth have asked to become covenant member of All Souls Church. We will celebrate their full membership on Sunday. The other joy is that there is to be a marriage. Jason Goulet and Monica Ashworth-Twist have asked for the blessing of the church." Everyone clapped and cheered. "Now let us pray."

After grace was said I announced the menu.

"We have turkey and ham. There is also a Thanksgiving lentil loaf for those vegetarians among us. Many of our church members have brought their favorite side dishes so there is a great variety of wonderful food. There will be food for leftovers and you should all feel free to eat as much as you want. The buffet line is now open!"

People started forming a line at the buffet. Out of the corner of my eye I saw Bill Simpson enter. He looked lost and lonely. I was glad to see Rhonda and Monica rush over to him with a hug and take him to their table.

When everyone had gone through the line my kitchen helpers and I loaded up our plates and sat for dinner. Tim had saved me a seat next to him. Bill was safely seated between Rhonda and Monica. Jason and Monica were seated together as was Rhonda and Jackson.

Tim took my hand and gave it a squeeze. "You've done a good thing," he said as he looked around. Looking around the room and at the people at my table I knew I had much to be thankful for.

"There's no place like home!" I said to no one in particular.

A Midcoast Murder

Recipes from Jesse's Recipe Box.

In college in the 1970's, Jesse began to collect old church and community cookbooks from Maine. Restricted by a limited student budget, Jesse sought out recipes that were thrifty as well as flavorful. Many of the old recipes came from a time when great food variety was limited. Maine cooks were creative and managed to feed their families with few ingredients and fewer financial resources. Jesse has adapted many of these recipes, some which go back to colonial days, to reflect today's higher health consciousness.

Jesse has a few rules about ingredients. In baking, always use real butter and real vanilla extract, never margarine or imitation vanilla. Use meat and chicken sparingly, and when you do use it, try to obtain farm-raised organic meat, or free range poultry. The higher cost will be offset by the better flavor, and you will be supporting the small family farms, and not supporting the inhumane factory-farming agribusinesses.

Stephen E. Stanley

Shepherd's Pie

This one-dish meal originates from England, where Shepherd's Pie refers to a dish made with lamb, and the American beef version is called Cottage Pie. Jesse was first introduced to the dish in the school lunch program, which inexplicitly called it Chinese Pie.

1 lb. of ground beef
1 cup of cooked, diced carrots.
1 cup of cooked peas
1 small onion
1 can of creamed corn
1 small can of whole corn
1 cup of water or broth
3 tbs of flour
salt and pepper

Brown one pound of ground beef with one chopped onion. Season with salt and pepper. Once brown add the carrots and peas. Add one cup of water and flour and bring the meat mixture to a boil. Place the meat mixture in the bottom of a casserole dish. Place the creamed corn in a layer over the meat mixture and add the whole corn on top. Top the dish with mashed potatoes and place in a 350 degree oven for 35 minutes, or until the top of the potatoes begin to brown.

Three Bean Casserole

This is an easy crock pot recipe for a busy day.

1 package frozen lima beans
6 links mild Italian sausage, sliced
1 can kidney beans, rinsed
1 can white beans, rinsed
1 small onion, chopped
one green pepper, sliced
1 can tomato sauce
salt and pepper

Place all ingredients into the pot and cook on low for six to eight hours.

Beef Burgundy Casserole

An easy and flavorful beef dish to serve over egg noodles.

Preheat oven to 300 degree

1 lb. lean chuck cut into cubes
½ cup red wine
1 can beef consommé
salt and pepper
1 chopped onion
¼ cup bread crumbs
¼ cup flour
3 carrots, sliced thick

Mix all together, cover and bake for three hours

Stephen E. Stanley

Cola Meatloaf
Cola gives this meatloaf a sweet flavor

1 tbs mustard	1 tbs ketchup
1 chopped onion	1 cup bread crumbs
1 cup cola	1 lb ground beef

 Add more cola or breadcrumbs until you get the right consistency Place in a loaf pan and bake at 350 degrees for 45-60 minutes.

Bubble and Squeak

This is an English recipe that uses leftovers to create a hearty meal. There are a great many variations, but the most common elements are potato and cabbage. Here is Jesse's version. Depending on your leftovers, this will be a different dish every time.

1 cup of beef, pork, ham, of chicken, cut up into cubes.
1 cup of diced cooked potatoes
1 cup of shredded cabbage
Leftover peas, carrots, or corm
Any other leftovers you wish to add

Place ingredients into a well-greased fry pan. Fry until the potatoes begin to brown up.

Home-made Mayo

This is a very old recipe used for lobster salad and egg salad. It comes from a time before commercial mayo was readily available. It is a great addition to macaroni salads.

1 ½ tbs sugar	dash pepper
1 tsp salt	1 tsp dry mustard
1 tbs flour	1 beaten egg
¾ cups milk	¼ cup vinegar
2 tbs butter	

Mix all ingredients together in the top of a double boiler. Set the mixture over boiling water. Stir until thick. Removes from heat. Add the butter and stir. Place in the refrigerator for at least two hours.

Two-minute Key Lime Pie.

A tasty pie when you don't have the time or the inclination to make a multi-step dessert.

2 cans sweetened condensed milk
½ cup lime juice
One graham cracker pie shell.

Mix sweetened condensed mix and lime juice together until it begins to thicken. Place in pie shell, chill and serve with whipped cream.

Stephen E. Stanley

Quick Lemon Cheese Cake

Another time-saving dessert.

1 package of cream cheese
1 can lemon pie filling
1 graham cracker pie shell

Whip room-temperature cream cheese until fluffy, add lemon pie filling and whip until combined and fluffy. Put in pie shell and refrigerate. Serve with whipped cream.

Banana Muffins

Jesse often brings muffins to work. This is one of his favorites.

2 eggs	½ cup molasses
2 cups of flour	2 tsp baking power
¼ cup of oil	1 tsp vanilla
1 tsp salt	2 ripe bananas
1/8 cup sugar	

Mix ingredients and bake at 400 degrees for 25 minutes.

Cornmeal Biscuits

These biscuits are especially good with soups, stews, and chowders.

1 ½ cups unbleached flour
½ cup cornmeal   1 tbs baking powder
½ tsp salt   5 tbs butter
¾ milk   preheat oven to 425 degrees

Mix all dry ingredients and cut in the cold butter. Add milk and stir. Knead dough and cut into biscuits. Bake 12-15 minutes.

Carrot Ring

A great visual side dish for a buffet.

1 lb carrots sliced and cooked
1 small onion
3 tbs milk
1 tbs butter
1 tsp salt
3 beaten eggs

Mash and mix all ingredients and place in oiled ring mold. Set mold in a pan of water and bake at 350 degrees for forty minutes. Unmold onto a plate and serve with cooked peas in the middle.

Stephen E. Stanley

Made in the USA
Lexington, KY
24 July 2011